the DECEMBER BOYS

Michael Noonan is the author of eighteen novels and works of non-fiction for both adult and younger readers, including the well known *Flying Doctor* series, *Magwitch* and *A Different Drummer*. He is also a scriptwriter and playwright for radio, television, films and the stage. His works have been published, produced and broadcast internationally. His first book, *In the Land of the Talking Trees*, was written while he was on active service in New Guinea with the AIF during World War II. His teenage novel *McKenzie's Boots* (listed as one of the Best Books for Young Adults for 1988 by the American Library Association) draws on that wartime experience. *The Patchwork Hero* was a prize-winning ABC television serial. Like *The December Boys*, it is set in the 1930s. Both *McKenzie's Boots* and *The Patchwork Hero* are also published by the University of Queensland Press.

After the war, Michael Noonan studied art at the National Gallery, Melbourne (he is the author of a biographical novel about the painter Turner, *The Sun Is God*), then drama, literature, history and philosophy at the University of Sydney. From 1957 to 1979 he lived in England, returning to Australia to make his home in Queensland.

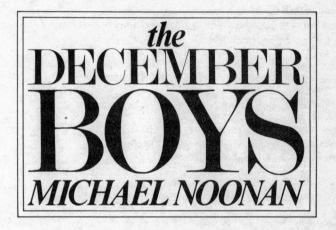

the
DECEMBER
BOYS
MICHAEL NOONAN

University of Queensland Press

First published 1963 by William Heinemann, London
Revised edition published 1990 by University of Queensland Press
Box 42, St Lucia, Queensland 4067 Australia

Typeset by University of Queensland Press
Printed in Australia by The Book Printer, Maryborough

Distributed in the USA and Canada by
International Specialized Book Services, Inc.,
5602 N.E. Hassalo Street, Portland, Oregon 97213-3640

Arts for
Australians
Australia Council

Creative writing program assisted by
the Literature Board of the Australia
Council, the Federal Government's arts
funding and advisory body

Cataloguing in Publication Data
National Library of Australia
Noonan, Michael, 1921- .
  The December boys.

  I. Title. (Series : UQP young adult fiction).

A823.3

ISBN 0 7022 2293 3

*To Ted Willis, under whose baronial roof
this story was conceived, for his long years
of friendship and encouragement.*

AUTHOR'S NOTE

The December Boys is set in the 1930s, before the outbreak of the Second World War. The economic Depression of the early 1930s hit Australasia especially hard; the deserted camp and the boarded-up caves the boys discover at Captain's Folly were typical of a number of temporary dwelling places set up by the jobless and destitute.

1 "Have you anything more to confess, my son?"
    The husky whisper came from the dark shape behind the metal grille, the head of the priest.

Yes, I had but I was having trouble getting it off my chest.

So far my sins had been routine and unspectacular: swear words; the name of Jesus Christ taken in vain; laughing in church; telling lies about washing my feet at night, and behind my ears; morning and evening prayers ignored. Yet I felt I had an excuse for abandoning prayer since I was already treading the strands of what seemed tantamount to anyone's paradise — Roman Catholic, Protestant or whatever.

"Speak up, my son."

How could I explain? It was no fault of mine that I had come by the information. It had been thrust on me, a sort of forbidden fruit. Yet I had been given no choice but to partake of it.

"I've got a secret," I said at last.

"A secret, my son?"

"Yes, Father."

"And it troubles you?"

"Yes, Father."

"Perhaps you have been tempted by bad thoughts?"

My acquaintance with the world of the flesh had not yet begun in the way that he suggested, but I had most certainly been having bad thoughts of a kind. In fact, for some ten days my life had been one long bad thought. The information I had overheard was precious, and I had been obsessed with thinking how to stop it from reaching the sunburnt ears of my four companions."

"A secret can be a sin, my son."

I was afraid of that.

"It will ease your mind to unburden yourself?"

1

So I told him. I revealed how I had been an eavesdropper, quite unintentionally, to a conversation between a man named Fearless Foley and another called Shellback O'Leary, and how the woman Teresa was involved.

It set him a problem not frequently posed by a customer aged just twelve. He pondered in that curtained box where the dark birds of conscience were uncaged and vanquished. As I knelt in the confessional, the silence outside was choked with prayer. It was broken only by the clatter of the forgiven and the about-to-be-forgiven in and out of the pews.

"My son," came the whisper, "in keeping this knowledge to yourself are you being fair to the others? By remaining silent it is possible that you are being selfish, and that in itself can be sinful in the eyes of God. Surely, then, for your own peace of mind it would be best for you to tell the other boys all that you overheard. Share the secret with them, my son. The good things of life, and the burdens, are all the better if they are shared."

He droned absolution in mumbo Latin. Penance seemed to range in those days from three Hail Marys to a decade of the Rosary, depending on the frequency and magnitude of sin confessed. I was spared this, but I knew enough about my religion to understand that the cleansing of my soul would not be final until I had carried out the priest's prescription and given those eight sunburnt ears something to set them tingling.

"Pray for me, my son," he murmured as he slid a wooden panel across the grille and opened up for business on the other side of the box.

Pray for him? Surely, after having been set this task, I was going to be busy enough praying for myself.

2 Just over two weeks earlier we had come to the place called Captain's Folly and looked down on the sea (and the scene of my unwitting sin) for the first time in our lives.

We had nine eyes between us for the event, nine good eyes, all as bright as quicksilver that morning: the usual two apiece for Spark, Maps, Fido and me, one only for Misty. His right eye did not work properly and he kept it hidden behind a clouded spectacle pane.

Until now the earth's surface had been pieces of pie-crust shaped like continents and islands, all surrounded by water. Not ordinary water. Water with power: the power to inspire men to sea-shanties; the power to cast others away under lone palm trees while it took years to deliver their bottled messages back to civilisation. And what a wonder it was. Sheer immensity. Sky distilled to liquid. As we stood on a hilltop yellowed by summer, it was a Friday morning, and our sockless toes curled and flared in our Sunday boots.

"There it is, boys," said Mrs McAnsh. "The Pacific."

"That's right. The Specific," murmured her husband, introducing us to the odd distorted echoes of her statements that became more pronounced when he had been imbibing.

Our glimpses of the sea up to this time had been highly artificial. There was the oil-painting in the visitors' room at St Roderick's, a murky seascape freckled with full stops dropped by the outback version of the common house-fly, and at one time or another we had all fixed our eyes on it while married couples decided that their childless lives were not so dismally unfulfilled after all. Now not a single fly-spot marred our view. Only the hovering motes of our own dizziness lay bet-

3

ween us and a gloss that was the glaze off a billion beautiful blue-green tiles.

No glimpse had prepared us for this. Certainly not the azure pond behind Our Lady Star of the Sea in the big print in the chapel at St Roderick's. That was a dull imitation. Nor were the travel posters around the railway station equal to what confronted us now, no matter how tantalisingly their headlands and their surf had beckoned to us through the heat-waves that pulsed off the bricks.

Fido, much the smallest of the five of us, so slight that his bones might have been thin steel rods and fence wire, now had one of his seizures.

"Crumbs!" he twanged. "It's gotta fire under it."

"A fi-er?"

The crack-voiced warble came from behind us, from the knuckle-ankled, double-shafted, black-frocked stand for a hat that looked like a secondhand wreath, the petals of its satin roses dog-eared, flattened and faded.

"A fi-er?" repeated Mrs McAnsh, the female section of the kind couple in whose charge we were to be. *"Under* it?"

"Lady, just look!" cried Fido, skin and fence wire trembling down at the snowy flummeries that clumped into shape and rolled, shrinking, to the sand. "It's on the boil! Boilin' over! Gotta fire under it!"

Hullo, I thought, Fido could be right. This so-called sea is molten glass frothing along the edge. It's hot up here, too. That's why.

The male hatstand spoke up: "Upon my wretched soul, Cynthia, this time we surely have a bright lot of distress signals in our safekeeping."

Distress signals! Us? What did he mean by that, this ageing hatstand?

4

He had thick bow legs to upholster baggy trousers that wrinkled over unpolished brown boots. His moustache was untrimmed and untrained and grinned on behalf of the mouth it partly hid. His hat looked as if it might have a lively hard-luck story to tell. For instance, it could have been blown a hundred miles across the sharp edges of a stony desert, then carried out to sea, sodden, salted, hurled ashore, there to be snatched up by a crazy beachcomber of a dog, shaken and wrenched, perforated by teeth and abandoned at death's door. The brim drooped all around and looked as if it would collapse altogether when the sun worked up to its full thump.

Another of the alleged distress signals fluttered. It was Misty this time.

" 'Sa flood!" he yelled suddenly. "A flood!" He lapsed into the sort of talk we heard from the stock saleyards next door to St Roderick's. "It's the biggest damned almighty flood ever there was!"

"Upon my very wretched soul!" muttered Mr McAnsh.

"Language! Language!" cried his wife — at us, of course.

Mr McAnsh used a cuff to wipe the mouth of a bottle of ruby wine and handed it to his wife. A swig left her short of breath. "Come along, boys," she gasped. "Come along down."

"Up down," muttered the other hatstand.

Mrs McAnsh's ankles wobbled as she trod over the rubble surface. Perhaps a nut in them wanted tightening, or a race of ball-bearings needed replacing. As we followed, Mr McAnsh shoved the wine-bottle in his hip pocket. It poked up through the cloth of his jacket and wagged at us like a sly forefinger.

3 Spark became vocal as we reached the end of the first leg of the zigzag road.

Probably the briny smell of the sea triggered it, somehow reminding him of the pungent animal odours that swamped through our classrooms and lingered in the dormitory on sale days. Sheep and cattle were sold once a week, and sometimes wild horses and goats. The bawling jangle of the auctioneers intrigued him, and one day he planned to join them. He was the only one of us certain of what he wanted to be; he was sure it would come to pass, and we believed so, too. He often imagined himself on an auctioneer's rostrum, and he had trial runs without anything particular to sell, indulging in a sort of inarticulate warming up, a flexing of his vocal cords, a performance akin to the *do-re-mi* wails of the choir ladies who came to St Roderick's for what were supposed to be singing lessons.

Down the stretch of road he went. "Hurrum! Hoo! Hee! Haw! Haw-hah! Haw-hah! Boing, boing! Bong! Old!" All of which we took to mean: "One hundred! Two! Three! Four! Four and a half! Four and a half! Going, going! Gone! Sold!"

Spark was ginger and well freckled, his eyes milky blue. On a visit to St Roderick's the bishop had asked him what he did before going to sleep every night. Spark gave a prompt and canny reply: "I pray for the Pope." The bishop chortled and said that here was a bright spark, and thus a nickname was born.

We picked up the cheap suitcases containing our few belongings, and in the wake of the McAnshes and the wagging wine-bottle we descended into the mouth of a valley that ran into the sea. The formation was that of a headless torso, arms divided, wrists scarred by cliffs, and hands dipped into the ocean. At the foot of a steep hillside opposite were two cottages, one painted light blue, its garden ablaze with a species of ice-plant that opens by day and encrusts the ground in silken-surfaced sheaths of deep scarlet, magenta, buttercup, lavender and tangerine. Here and elsewhere on the hillside it was in patches so dense and glistening that each might have been some exotic tapestry laid out in the sunlight. The other cottage was white, its path marked by white-washed stones, and in its garden was a phrase picked out in bleached shells:

THERE IS
NO JUSTICE

Another leg of the road took us to a point from which the full sweep of the beach lay revealed: sandhills with long grasses faintly tinged with green, dry yellow sand pocked like pewter, darker damp sand, smooth, except for a lone set of footprints down to the water.

The line of these footprints took our eyes out through the waves to something that was bobbing towards the shore. A red ball? No, we saw a face under it. Someone was riding in with a wave. Presently, in the shallows, where the foam wove brief patterns of lace, a figure in a glistening green bathing-costume rose to her feet.

At a distance toddlers recognise fellow toddlers, small boys other small boys, dogs other dogs. We saw at once that this creature from the sea was a grown woman. She splashed through the thin foam to the wet sand, where she laid a second set of footprints. She used both hands to press the water down over her breasts and hips, and then she tugged off the red bathing-cap, letting loose a small flaxen shower that settled over her shoulders, until she brushed its flow to the back of her neck. She crumpled the bathing-cap as she walked and threw it up the beach. She moved forward at a run, checking herself with a slight dancing hop, and then she executed what must always be the most perfect and most beautiful cartwheel I have ever seen. She hung momentarily upside down on the palms of her hands, her hair touching the sand; then her hair streamed back over her shoulders as the cartwheel landed her on her feet again. What a treat for our nine eyes. The distance seemed to make that cartwheel exquisitely slow, and every phase of it is impressed on my mind, a flower preserved with its original brightness between pages of memory.

Such was our first glimpse of Teresa.

She was beside the bathing-cap now and stooped to pick it up. As she reached the soft sand her walk changed, each step becoming a sort of downward jab. It puzzled us why she should suddenly seem to be marching, but we were soon to learn that the dry sand could retard footsteps and that this walk made crossing it easier. She was a grown woman, as we had been quick to decide, but that cartwheel seemed to tell us that part of her was still somewhere in our world.

The two hatstands were making fast time downhill and we hurried along after them, the ice-plants like brilliant banners opposite, the sea booming chords of greeting, and some two months of freedom ahead — a freedom which, because the means of an even greater escape was dangled in front of us, we were doomed to abuse.

4 Our bathing-costumes were designed and fashioned by the nuns in the workrooms at St Roderick's, but Old Nick had apparently taken a hand in their making, despite the presence of holy pictures and medals and other religious items that might have been expected to

warn him off. They were cut from flour-bags and dyed black. The brand marks were still faintly discernible, and some of us wore them to the front, some to the back, as we trooped down from the McAnsh head-quarters to inspect those feminine footprints. They were still the only marks on the wet sand, and since the tide was going out there was now a gap between the point where they ended and the edge of the water.

In a sense our bodies bore brands. We were burnt by the outback sun, but only in parts. Our skin was pallid above the knees, around the neck and shoulders, and above the elbows, and the black of the costumes sharpened the whiteness as we stopped beside the foot-prints.

"Hasn't got very big dogs," observed Spark, fitting a foot into the outline in the sand. He had caught this expression from Sister Ursula, who was always telling us that her poor old dogs were barking. She had bad bun-ions, yet outwardly she was the happiest nun, and since she could be cheerful even though suffering we came to regard her as the only truly saintly woman in the convent.

"Got wallopin' big 'ands, though," said Fido, as usual dropping the tail of one word and the head of another, as he went down on his knees to spread his thin fingers like crow's feet in the imprint of one of the hands.

"She must have got herself left behind," said Misty.

Our demands for enlightenment overlapped.

"Left behind?" " 'Ow?" "When?" "You're barmy!"

"By the circus."

"Whatcha talkin' about?" "What circus?"

"She must be one of them acrobats. Probably from a circus. Got herself left behind."

"Arr, you've got some of your behind stuck where your brains ought to be!" jeered Maps.

No one took up Misty's theory. He had been obsessed by circuses ever since the Rotary gentlemen took us to a matinee of the circus that had stayed a week at the rear of the saleyards. I remember it mainly because the local kookaburras used to start their cackling at the first wink of dawn, and from the racket let loose by the lions it was clear that the noblest of beasts took the jackass laughter as some sort of Antipodean insult.

Spark examined a footprint nearer the water. "Haw! She's got corns!"

"Whereabouts?"

"You got eyes!"

With his forefinger Spark whisked inside the curve at the base of the big toe. There was a distinct bump in the imprint, but how could the feet of a person capable of such a supple and carefree cartwheel be marred by corns of any consequence? Spark was being disdainful just to avoid any suggestion that he had been impressed by anyone of the female sex. We had heard him already in the sleeping-hut adjoining the McAnsh cottage as we changed into bathing-costumes: "All she was doing was shaking the ants out of her hair."

Corns or no corns, we followed the footprints down to where they finished, and then we stood facing the sea.

Dare we venture into it so soon?

"C'mon! C'min!" yelled Maps. He had the sharpest voice among us, and in fact he was the sharpest in looks and in ways. His nickname had arisen from his early habit of peering into atlases and slowly tracing routes across land and ocean with his finger. Thus he had a certain acquaintance with the sea and had reason to lead us into it.

We advanced behind him into the shallows where the

10

stampeding high-dazzlers of waves feebly hissed their last. We fingered the water with our toes, curling them, sheathing our feet and ankles in cool transparent boots. The water magnified and distorted our toenails and they wiggled up at us even when we did not move them. There were many times when we shared the same emotion, and this was one of them. We were deeply aware of the ocean's might, its beauty and its mystery, as we moved farther into it, little by little, letting out cries of mingled fright and ecstacy as the first waves struck our shins and the leaping spray speckled our bathing-costumes with wetness. It roared out enough sound of the sea to fill thousands of shells, and we shouted against it.

"It's fizzin' like lemonade!"

"Pity there isn't a fire under it. I'm froze."

"It's mad!"

"Hey, it tastes like holy water!"

"Wow, it's strong. It's trying to push me over!"

This was our first communion with a great entity. God had created the world and its waters, yet was not the sea in its turn responsible for the existence of so much else? For the exploits of Vasco da Gama, Magellan, Columbus, Sir Walter Raleigh? Without the sea what reason would we have for remembering these adventurers? It was responsible for trade winds, Trafalgar, pirates and press gangs, the fingerprint whorls of ocean currents on world maps, the giant hair of the Sargasso, the *Flying Dutchman* and the *Fighting Temeraire,* jellyfish, flying fish, whales, sharks, the confusion over the plural spelling of the octopus and the trials of trying to rattle off *She sells seashells on the seashore . . .*

Maps took the first plunge, backing into a wave and sitting down in its path, his guarded eyes all staring for

11

once, his cockscomb of black hair briefly enveloped in an outsize Dominican cowl. He vanished for some moments, then stood up blowing hard, his hair flattened, his bathing-costume stuck to his body like a skin of new lacquer. One by one we dipped ourselves, Misty taking care to keep his head well clear of the water, and soon we were all spluttering and hollering, so much so that we collected a small audience.

Above the rocks either side of the bay there were ledges, and above these were shacks half-built into the cliff-face, making homes out of caves. On the left was a yellow-fronted shack, and set against this background was a squat, bald man with skin the colour of vinegar, roomy shorts dangling at an angle from his hips, and his hands forming a double brim over his eyes. To the right, in front of a shack painted grey and partly glassed-in, was a lean, tall man, who smoked a pipe and seemed to be slowly unlimbering the joints in the fingers of his free hand. And on the beach, a little down from the gap in the sandhills, the cartwheel lady was watching us, a wide-brimmed hat on her head. The McAnshes had warned us not to go too far out into the surf, and as we began to withdraw so did the three watchers.

Misty was first to leave, partly because a splash hit his spectacles, partly because his fingers had become bloodless and cold. The rest of us were close behind him. I mentioned that Old Nick had been in on the making of our bathing-costumes. He was due to have a most satisfying time in Captain's Folly. Now was his first chance to smirk behind the prongs of his pitchfork. The water around us seemed to be dusky. We were emanating blackness. And as we came out of the water and onto sand we found that the dye was running, striping our legs.

This was not the only humiliation. The flour-bags

were holding water. We floundered around with its dead weight caught in the backsides.

"Hey, look! We've been turned into bumble-bees!" yelled a delighted Sparks.

Fido let go a few thin chirps of laughter. Misty was terrified. I think Maps must have suspected some Satanic conspiracy, and I remember being embarrassed. But, as the water drained away down our legs, there was no one watching, except an aged grey horse not far from that yellow-fronted shack. In the workrooms at St Roderick's the nuns might be experts at making gorgeous vestments for the priests and turning out exquisite embroidery, but they were poor hands at bathing-costumes.

Hot sand soaked up the wetness as we settled ourselves near the mobile life-saving reel, a sort of two-wheeled chariot, all ready for use with its canvas belt balanced on top of what looked like a mile of strong bleached cord. Our feet were towards the sea, and up in front of us was the weatherboard pavilion with a painted notice under the eaves:

CAPTAIN'S FOLLY
SURF AND LIFE-SAVING CLUB

The thud of the waves came up through the beach under us. To me it was a great fist wearily pounding to emphasise something it had been preaching for aeons, something to do with fate or destiny, some stern warning. I did not view the sea in terms of a flood, nor could I imagine that there was a fire under it. I was wary of it and reminded of something, but as yet I had not defined what that might be. At least it was not the clutching monster that Sister Agnes had warned us to expect.

She was a lay nun, one of the black-aproned worker bees in that stern hive, and she had entered the convent

13

as an act of thanksgiving after being rescued in her girlhood from drowning.

What girlhood? We were entitled to ask that. It was beyond any of us to believe that the shrivelled and desolate beak poking out of that starched white wimple had ever glowed with the pink of youth. It was a thing of stale and hardened putty. It could never have been young enough to twitch at the fragrances of, say, its eleventh summer. And what an odd way to react to being rescued, committing oneself to a lifetime behind those joyless stone walls. If Sister Agnes was capable of such imbalance, then surely her views on the sea were open to doubt.

About the time we were brushing chunks of dry sand off our fronts, Fido suddenly curled up on knees and elbows. He was the first of us to spot the cartwheeling woman coming at that jabbing walk through the gap in the sandhills. She wore the same green bathing-costume, dry now and without any glisten, and balanced on her head was the wide-brimmed hat, of untinted straw with a cluster of knotty flowers made of raffia. We were able to identify the material because we used it at St Roderick's to make napkin rings that were sold at church bazaars or given as presents to patrons.

Sand spurted with each jab of her feet, happy feet, with bulges at the bases of her big toes certainly, but definitely no ungainly corns. She carried a bottle of thick liquid, cloudy and pink, and a smile began at the corners of her mouth as she stopped and looked down at us as we rose by way of hands and knees onto our feet.

"Who's the boss here?" she asked, singing it a little, making it a musical question.

We hesitated. We were not a gang with a recognised leader. We were lumped together and known as "the December boys" because it was believed our birthdays

were in the same calendar month. If we were to choose a
leader, it would be either Spark or Maps.

"Never mind, I'll be boss. Line up."

What did she mean by this?

"Look at those shoulders," she said. "You'll burn
yourselves red raw. Line up. That's the idea. Now who's
first? You'll do. Just stand still."

Maps had this honour. He narrowed his eyes when
foxed or on guard, and they were like that now, while
his top lip was cocked up to one side in a startled half-
smile, half-grimace. Teresa shook the bottle and held
the screw-on stopper between her teeth as she poured
some of the pink liquid into the shallow of her palm and
slapped it over Maps's shoulders and began to spread it.
Fido was wrong about her hands. They seemed an
appropriate size for a grown woman and no more. They
had something of the grace in their movements of that
first cartwheel. Her breasts quivered as she rubbed, and
her skin, although a seasoned brown over her shoulders
and most of her arms and legs, was a honey tan around
her throat and on her face. Her hair hung either side,
paler than her high cheeks, and her eyes were a different
hue to the hard jade of her bathing-costume, a sort of
liquid golden-green.

"Where are you kids from?" she asked, trying to
speak with the stopper between her lips.

"S'int Roderick's."

She seemed to realise that we were a little dismayed by
the way the stopper distorted her speech — to say
nothing of the shape of her lips — so she gave it to Maps
to hold while she started on Spark. From nervousness he
began to gabble. Far from asserting that he knew that
she was left over from a circus, he began to inform her
how we had travelled all yesterday by train after a dawn
start and had arrived in the city shortly before another

dawn when the big station was clanging with the sound of milk-cans being unloaded, and how we had mounted a bus and finished the journey cross-country to be met at a lonely stop by Mr and Mrs McAnsh. Misty was next, but Spark kept rattling out the talk. It was our first look at the sea, he said. We were here by courtesy of the titled lady who lived up there on the hill in the mansion that was enclosed by a high wall and topped by a glassed-in turret-room, itself topped by the gold glint of a weather-vane.

"That's Lady Hodge," said Teresa. Without being told she knew what we were and why we were here.

"Yes, and she's paying for our fares and our eats."

"You kids sure could do with a good feed," she said, completing the oiling of Misty and grasping my shoulder. "You're all just skin and bone."

The sunburn lotion was smooth and cool and strongly perfumed. The hills shimmered before my eyes as Teresa rubbed. I was afraid that I might somehow become magnetised. I had once seen someone rub the composition holder of an Eversharp pencil on rough cloth and so give it the power to make confetti-sized pieces of paper fly to it and stay stuck there. Too much of this rubbing and I would repeat that sort of thing on a much larger scale. Just a few scraps of newspaper lay half-buried, but perhaps they would break loose from the pocked dry sand and hurtle at me and paper me all over. Near the pavilion there was a noticeboard on a pole carrying a printed sheet of the by-laws of the district. It was curling away at the top corners and it, too, might come flying through the air to hit me between the eyes with the regulations (ignored by all) stating that mixed bathing was prohibited and that costumes must cover the body entirely from neck to knee. Meanwhile, I felt I was being anointed, receiving a sacrament not listed among the seven in our catechism, a sacrament that brought about a sort of investiture in a new life, the direct opposite of the Extreme Unction given at the time of death.

Fido jumped his turn by bolting.

"Quickly!" cried Teresa. "Grab him! Bring him back!"

Spark and Maps saw to this, catching Fido near the notice and dragging him on his behind so that he left a long gutter in the sand.

He remained in a sitting position for his oiling, but under Teresa's touch he became pathetically tame. He just stared up at her and responded with a quick, goofy grin each time she smiled at him. He lifted a smear of the lotion with the tip of a forefinger and sniffed its perfume. He was the most likely lap-dog amongst us: he had been nicknamed after the mosquito-like pet dog in a comic strip.

"Why'd you do that cartwheel?" he sprang with innocence.

"A cartwheel?"

"When you come outa the water?"

"Did I?"

"Did'n she?" Fido whirled on us for support, and we all nodded a grave agreement.

"Well, I expect I did. Yes, of course! I always feel like doing cartwheels on Friday."

She laughed as if amused at herself for having such an enchanting eccentricity. She took the stopper from Maps and screwed it back on to the bottle.

"Don't stay too long in the sun today. Tomorrow I'll give you another dose all round." She pointed through the gap in the sandhills to what we had already identified as a combined shop and cottage. "You'll find me up there. If I don't seem to be around, just ring the bell, or bang the counter. 'Bye now."

Her fingertips glistened with oil and she twinkled them at us and started up the beach, her flaxen hair jogging over her shoulders under the straw hat, while the calves of her legs — with the same fresh tint as her cheeks — quivered like her breasts.

For the second time she had taken us by surprise. The cartwheel had drawn us to her. The sunburn lotion was a transparent net that had captured us.

5 On that first day in Captain's Folly we took Teresa's advice and did not expose our shoulders too long in the sun. In fact we protected ourselves with some shade from the bed of the ocean.

At the south end of the beach was a mass of seaweed with huge rubbery leaves and translucent branches as thick as our ankles and wrists. We carved into both leaves and branches with the small pocket-knives given to us by the nuns as Christmas presents. The handles were engraved with the name of the produce merchant who supplied St Roderick's with bran and shell-grit for the orphanage fowls — fowls whose eggs were mainly mythical, if we were to judge from the glimpses we had of them.

Each leaf cut up easily. Between the two leathery surfaces was sandwiched a thickness of yellow cells like the insides of crumpets. We made triangular hats, slitting up through the cells and opening the seaweed so that we could plant the hats on our heads. We tried leggings to cover our shins, flap-like shoes, then jerkins and armbands and aprons, until we looked like some warriors of the Dark Ages preparing for combat. We armed ourselves with weapons whittled from seaweed branches, wobbling swords and drunken truncheons.

Arrayed thus, and carrying with us the pungent ozone smell of the mutilated seaweed, we advanced along the beach in the early afternoon to find out why that slow-moving grey horse was acting in such a strange way. It was splashing about in the shallows at the northern end of the beach, near that yellow-fronted shack half-built into a cave, higher on the hillside now that the outgoing tide had left more rock exposed below it.

Someone cried out: "That horse is biting the water!"

Another snapped a caution: "Shuddup!"

We watched in silence from under the quivering peaks of our seaweed hats as the horse splashed down at the water with one fore-hoof and then snapped just under the surface, its lips pulled back over fence-paling teeth. It repeated the splash of the hoof and the bite. A third time, and when it lifted its head we saw a silver bit wriggling between its teeth. A live silver bit.

" 'Ey! Lookit! That 'orse! It's fishin' without no 'ooks!"

The seaweed swords and truncheons drooped at our sides as we watched the grey horse clop through the thin water to the rocks, the fish held in its teeth. It dropped the catch onto the flat surface of a rock, but its hoof was simultaneously poised to strike, and it stamped down, leaving the fish lifeless. It backed away and looked up to the tufts of grass in the clay hillside above the rocks.

A small dark head eased into view. It was carried out on a long, slowly-extending neck. Then the full cat emerged, black with white markings, its tail bushed.

It came down a yard at a time, halting to watch the horse, and then us. Behind it, smaller black heads darted out and withdrew as quickly, three of them, kittens, offspring of this wild cat. It poised itself a few yards above the fish, that now lay with a ruby-red ooze coming from its crushed head. Suddenly a leap down, a flurried grab, a scuttle, a flash of silver, and the wild cat was soaring back to its hide-out in the tufts of grass and the trio of small black heads. A moment later all had vanished.

At such magic we reeled.

The grey horse turned towards the sea and stood as if puzzled by the neighs and whinnies of all those charging wild-horse waves. We broke into awed comment, only to have a raw brogue interrupt us from near the yellow-fronted shack: " 'Tis nothin' to be ravin' about! There's niver a day passes thit ye don't see thit same horse pilferin' fish from the ocean, jist t'give to thim wild felines.''

It was the tanned bald man in the dangling shorts.

What was wrong with him? An old horse catching fish for wild cats — if that happened a hundred times a day, surely it would still be a wonder!

Apparently this man did not think so. He padded along on the outer edges of bare pigeon-toed feet that later caused Spark to remark: "He's got dogs like old bush roots." A furze of bleached hair clung like a strange white light over his shoulders and his back. His eyes were a watery blue and the skin around them seemed to be tightening with age.

"Domestic cats gone wild," he informed us. "Hangovers from the days av the Depression. Jist like Socrates.''

Who might Socrates be, we asked.

"The devil be cursed, ye know Socrates, surely? Ye've seen him up to his daily trick, haven't ye jist?'' He pointed towards the horse, and we understood. "He wuz transported all the way up here be the boys who migrated from thit shanty town in the estuary av the city. They regarded him as some sort av philosopher, an' he wuz allowed t'dream most av the time, but now an'

20

thin he'd be called upon t'drag along a plough for the boys whan they had their gardens up there in the valley. At the time this place wuz burstin' with life.''

We had no trouble understanding him as the Reverend Mother at St Roderick's was Irish. ''Now,'' this man went on, ''I fear the place has had its day, and ye might jist as well know that from the start. Av course, whan we had the population, ivery day was a grand occasion. There were doctors an' lawyers av the land, men av letters an' learnin', all av thim here be the dozen. Now, alas, they've gone off in pursuit av prosperity. Ah, yis, 'twas a time, to be sure. A man could spend a whole day carvin' the initials av his name on the seat av thit bus-stop up on the top av the hill, an' thin stroll back as much as a week later to add the finishin' touches. I'm tellin' ye now, whativer ye imagine y'selves t'be in all thit seaweed muck, it takes a thing the like av a Depression t'make the soul av a man shine in his eyes.''

Though the content of his talk tended to bewilder us, we were intrigued by the volume of his delivery. He eyed us through shrinking button-holes of skin as he leaned with his hand against the rock and stood on one short leg to scratch behind the knee with the curled toe of his loose foot.

''I take it ye'er the lot stayin' up with Bandy McAnsh an' his missus?''

''Yes, mister,'' said Spark, seeking enlightenment. ''He called us the new lot of distress signals.''

''Distress signals?''

For a moment the man glowered with puzzlement. Then he showed two brown teeth to one side and plenty of well shrunken gum elsewhere as a preliminary to a hoarse laugh. ''Haha. So that's what he called ye, eh? Distress signals.'' Another laugh, but no explanation —

although after our first look around the McAnsh household we had a glimmering of its meaning. "Thim two, they're jist the pair t'give ye an expert lesson in how to live on ye wits, if ye're so inclined t'learn. Nivertheless, they've an aptitude fer livin'. Too manny of thim thit are left here are a drab an' dopey lot av halfbaked dreamers."

A chord of music crashed in the bay.

The man spun on his feet, and our heads spun too, as a piano began to play. But where? Where was it? The man's arm and clenched fist were raised towards the opposite side of the bay, and then we realised that the music was coming from the cave into which the lean pipe-smoker had withdrawn earlier.

"The mad galoot!" raged our aged cock-sparrow of an informant. "D'ye know what he's got there in thit cave av his? D'ye know what?"

"'Course," one of us ventured. "A piano."

"A *grand* piano."

Now we really were impressed.

"A great mouldy thing it is, I'll be bound. An' judgin' from all the tortured playin' thit comes out av it, there must be barnacles thick on the keyboard. There must be some good reason fer all thit unmelodious dirge, eh? There must be some reason for it."

He looked quickly to each of us for agreement, yet to us the music had a regal pomp, as if the rocks were responsible for it. "Av course, he's but wun av the idiots. There is, for instance, her ladyship up there in her eyrie, lightin' candles for the dead with five-pound banknotes. An' thin there's the nincompoop thit's been buildin' himself a boat these five years past. It's behind thim sandhills, under a black canopy av canvas, but the fella's here ivery week-end, hammerin' an' tappin' away, an' when the contraption is finished he's plannin' t'sail around the world, maniac thit he is. He's even gone as far as suggestin' t'me thit I might accompany him on the trip as part av his crew. I'm a seafarin' man meself, retired av course, but there's nothin' wrong with that. Me name's O'Leary and at the time av the Depression the boys took t'callin' me Shellback, and I've resigned meself to the name. — Listen, listen! What a pagan dirge it is! Even Socrates cannot abide that racket.''

The horse was meandering up the beach to some spot behind the sandhills. Yet he did not appear to be in any great desperation to escape from the echoing passages of piano music emanating from the cave, where double glass doors were open in the grey front.

''Oh, I tell ye, there's some odd ones here in the Folly, me boys.'' Shellback O'Leary thrust out a bent forefinger towards the cottage, where the shells in the front garden spelled out: THERE IS NO JUSTICE. ''What about thit half-wit?'' His finger rose higher, to a cottage overlooking the valley where its two sides began to join. ''And ole Watson with his witches' brew concocted from loganberries, parsnips, pumpkins an' the like. Poison it is, the lot av it, despite his own high opinions and his mistaken belief that it's entitled t'be called wine!''

If Shellback considered the piano-playing a dirge, then perhaps his judgment on the home-made concoctions might be astray, too. This old blowhard was fast establishing himself as a valuable source of local information and history. Yet one of our number was momentarily concerned with something else.

Misty had been carrying a stone. Now he decided to throw it into the water. Before it splashed, Shellback was wailing: ''Be all the saints, ye'll upset Henry!''

Misty's startled one eye asked who Henry might be,

while our remaining eight eyes joined him in the question.

"He's lurkin' out there near the wreck."

What wreck? we asked.

"The sailin' ship! How d'ye think this place came be its name? The skipper mistook this inlet for the heads av the city estuary. Must've bin a ravin' imbecile to make an elimintary mistake like that. Anyway, 'twas what happened, and now Henry's out there in the dimness thit surrounds the rottin' timbers av the ship. He's a giant groper, and since first I came here, an' that wuz eight years ago, I've bin pittin' me brains against his wiles. His taste in bait remains a mystery to me, although I've tried him with nigh on everythin' except a stick av lighted gelignite."

Before going on he lifted a hand in front of us. His fingernails were corrugated and discoloured like a type of tortoise-shell. "The brain av a fish is said t'be no bigger thin the tip av a man's little finger. Yet it's a long dance he's led me, the crafty divil thit he is."

A long dance, all right. Had he started a few years earlier, he could have claimed to have stalked that one fish for as long as we had been alive.

"Yet I'll git him, I will. I'll git him."

He eyed us as if we might be prospective baits. We began to edge back and Spark covered our withdrawal by asking a quick question: "How big's a groper, mister?"

"This wun's twice the size of you young desperadoes, twice the size. I'd mebbe stand a chance of landin' him this evenin', except Friday's always a bad night." He squinted up to the top of the hillside opposite, to the point from which we had taken our first look down into Captain's Folly, while we wondered again what might be so special about Friday. "It's always bad, with that

24

Fearless Foley tellin' the whole world about his arrival here.''

Who was Fearless Foley?

"Shades av pagan ignorance, ye've not heard av Fearless? Fearless Foley? Not a single wun av yer? Niver heard, an' here it is Friday!'' This time he pointed to the hilltop opposite. "On this day av the week, at the start av night-time, ginerally about an hour after the settin' av the sun, up there ye'll hear a wild roarin' as Fearless sits astride his Red Indian motor-bike, an' a monstrous machine it is. He's all arrayed in gloves, helmet, goggles, a great leather coat, an' proper leggin's.'' He sniffed down at our seaweed armour. "Down thit zigzag road he comes, just as though the handlebars av the machine were the wings av an aeroplane, explodin' with power, skiddin', backfirin', wavin' the light of his headlamp around like a great sword in the night. It's a matter av a very short time before all the suspince is over, but it's an age no doubt t'the young woman, his wife, and she happens t'be the same that slathered yer with protection against sunburn. It's a time whan all av us down here hold our breaths, and I'll admit to the fact thit I've caught meself whisperin' a prayer for the preservation av Fearless under me own breath.''

To merit such an honour, we thought, this Fearless Foley must be a mighty sort of man, a suitable husband to the young woman who had cartwheeled herself into our hearts. What a couple they must make!

Shellback had almost finished. "If you young desperadoes are not above takin' a word av advice, I'd not go paradin' around in all thit seaweed fer too long. It's liable to dry on ye so hard thit Bandy McAnsh will be obliged t'git busy with a hammer an' cold chisel t'set ye free!''

He started a dry laugh, but broke off to glare across the bay as the piano rose in a crescendo. He grabbed up a piece of iron and banged on a steel tyre-rim that hung near the yellow door. It failed to stop the piano, and it seemed that the bald clanging would be more likely than the other to upset the groper.

"I'll tell ye what thit fella does!" moaned Shellback. "Anny time I'm about t'hook thit monster av the deep, he strikes up an' batters away, an' after all these years Henry's come to recognise it as a warnin'. I'm up against diabolical competition!"

We left him to glower across the bay and drifted up the valley from the beach to inspect the red-leaded hull under the black canvas canopy. The seaweed armour began to grow clammy. We did not trust it now, so we discarded it piece by piece.

Mammoth shadows were thrown by the hills as the day came to an end. Despite them it had been essentially a day without shadow for us, and in this mood we began to build ourselves up for the arrival of Fearless Foley.

6 The McAnsh establishment consisted of a cottage and an adjoining sleeping-hut. Within its light-blue walls every day was a gala day because there were signal and national flags — and parts of them — everywhere. They were present as curtains, tablecloths, dishcloths, and they gave the place a jaunty cock-eyed air that was very much in keeping with the two owners.

Over our bunks in the sleeping-hut were signal flags as bedcovers, and once we were under them we had a better understanding of what Bandy meant when he called us distress signals — even though it was a weird association. Perhaps that hip-pocket wine-bottle had been trying to prepare us for something like this with its sly wagging.

Days later in the living-room we found a chart listing the meanings of the international code of signals, and discovered that we were sleeping under the squares and stripes of *Man Overboard, I Require a Pilot, I Have a Clean Bill of Health, I Am Carrying Mails.* Surely enough to touch off some lurid dreams.

Thanks to this same chart we identified one of the skirts worn by Mrs McAnsh as part of the flag for *My Engines Are Going Full Speed Astern.* Bandy popped his trombone nose into pieces of flag trimmed as handkerchiefs. We could not identify these, but judging from the warning blasts he blew they might have come from *Keep Clear of Me, I Am Manoeuvring with Difficulty.*

We dined on a tablecloth which was an old naval ensign, and after the meal we were introduced to our household duties, drying the dishes with pieces of flag. These were easy and pleasant tasks compared with those allotted to us at St Roderick's. They were not carried out under the same fear of punishment should there be any breakages. And not only breakages of crockery could be dangerous, as I well knew. At St Roderick's I had been detailed once to polish the floor in the main hallway, around the bottom of a big staircase, an area used only by the nuns and visitors. I had made too good a job of it. An elderly nun slipped and broke her hip, and I was transferred to peeling potatoes. Since that time I have had an understanding of the delicate formalities involved in what is known as diplomatic immunity. Nothing was said, there was no charge, no punishment, except that potato-peeling was one of the worst tasks. It was watched over by a sharp-eyed lay nun who complained that the shavings were wastefully thick if she could not see daylight through them.

Outside the McAnsh cottage the night slid down into the valley and poured out over the sea. We had heard darkness accompanied by the bawling of cattle and sheep, the baying of locomotive whistles and the percussion of couplings in the shunting yards, but darkness and the sob and whisper of the sea at night was a combination new to us. Through it we kept listening for the roar of Fearless Foley's motor-bike.

While we waited, the McAnshes introduced us to one of the consequences of their imbibing. (In her basket Mrs McAnsh had carried a number of companions to that wagging forefinger of a bottle.) She now went through the details of her first meeting with Bandy; their marriage, their wedded bliss. At least on the first occasion we were ready listeners to her account of her great romance.

"From the very start I was so impressed," she said, with a big smile at us, then a loving beam for Bandy. "It was the way he went about ordering his drink. First he raised his hat, and that was always a good sign in a well-run bar like mine. I caught myself all a-tremble at his courteous smile. Nothing such as this had happened to me in my life before, although I would dearly love to have as little as a sixpenny piece for every proposal I had across my bar counter.

"He kept coming in every day, walking all the way over the hill to Serenity just to be at my bar at Clarrity's Arms. Goodness, how I did feel for him walking back all on his own. By this time, of course, I had discovered what a fine person he was, and how he had such a very good position in charge of the garden on the Hodge property. Mr McAnsh was with her ladyship's late husband in the war, you know. His groom. Cavalry. Isn't that so, my love?"

"Every bit," nodded Bandy.

"Those were trying days for me, of course, wondering, as I was, what might become of our acquaintanceship. Then Mr McAnsh spent an entire afternoon in my bar, following which he was generous enough to stay on for the after-hours trading, and before that evening was concluded I found myself in the enviable position of being the prospective Mrs McAnsh. Isn't that right, my love?"

"Very bright," came the twisted echo.

"Well, now. I said it then — and I say it still — a man reveals his true nature in the way he takes his drink. There are those who cannot make up their minds what to have. The sippers are such finicky persons, the swallowers blunt and hard men. Mr McAnsh was that distinguished type who always knew what he wanted and invariably savoured what he had. He was a man who needed a prompt answer. No dithering for Mr McAnsh. So I gratefully said 'yes', and the banns were read, and our marriage was duly solemnised. And I might say that our mutual policy of take and give has rewarded us with five years of wedded joy so far. Isn't that so, Mr McAnsh? Live and let live, isn't that our way?"

"My word, indeed," he said. "Live and let love. That's us."

It was now suggested that it might be time for us to go to the sleeping-hut. There was no real insistence. We went there and changed into our convent-made pyjamas, and then we stood at the open doorway and looked across the sandhills to the top of the zigzag road. The bleating of the seagulls and a few drowned chords from the piano in the cave were mixed with the sound of the sea.

There were two false alarms. First, a car came down in tortured low gear. It brought the man who was building the boat on his weekends. A second car descended faster and drew up at the rear of the surf club pavilion, where some of the members of the life-saving team camped on Saturdays and Sundays. We waited on, the heat still beaming out of us into the soft darkness.

In the fevered high summer of the outback town we rarely went outside the walls of St Roderick's at this hour, only to some feast day procession in the town church, from which we came away with our clothing saturated with the smell of incense. Now we were shrouded in the smell of sunburn lotion and seaweed. The whole bay waited. Lights were on the alert behind the trees in front of the titled lady's mansion, in the cottage of the man said to make wine, and a lantern shone from Shellback's ledge. We had keyed ourselves up for something sudden and highly dramatic — explosive exhaust blasts, a headlamp beam flashing around like a long phosphorescent pennant in a mad wind. Yet all that came was a low drumming behind the crest of the hill and a pale cap of light.

Ah, but there was drama enough when Fearless broke out of the cocoon of hill and darkness. The drumming became a masterful pulse. A great glaring rod of light trembled out over the valley. The engine rose in frenzy, like some mechanical monster of an auctioneer unlimbering his voice for a sale which he knew would be a slaughter. Down he came, with the roar filling the valley and the bay and setting all the fragments of darkness jostling against one another and surely reaching into the sea to the lair of Henry the groper and other fish, big and little.

"He must be the wildest damned almighty man in the whole world!" Misty gasped.

The machine ripped down the inclines of the zigzag road. The engine screamed as it skidded on the bends, while the rear wheel sent rubble tumbling. The swinging beam of light slashed across our faces. That was a challenge, a slap on the cheek, a spit in the eye, and we abandoned the sleeping-hut and set out in pyjamas to the sandhills, reaching a high spot as the machine made its last turn and shot onto the flat and across to where Teresa waited outside the shop, drenching her in dancing light as she stood in a summer frock, skidding to a halt as she skipped a little to one side.

The engine coughed out and the headlamp died. A minute barking came from a dog somewhere in the Hodge property. A man's laugh, the deepest laugh any of us had ever heard, reached across to us, as a massive shape enclosed the paleness of Teresa's frock. A voice chimed richly: "Sweetheart, sweetheart!"

Fearless led her through the oblong of light that marked the doorway. He had to stoop and a loaded pack made a hump on his back.

The waves applauded. We were much too bewildered to join in.

Under the soles of our feet the surface of the sand was strangely dank, cool like petals, as if it lost its heat at night, in the way that the ice-plant flowers closed with the going of the sun.

We crept over to where the motor-bike stood, its rear wheel propped on an iron stand. It was faintly alive with the clicking sounds of withdrawing heat, although the cylinders remained so hot that when Spark spat on one of them there was an instant sizzle and a wisp of steam.

We took turns at spitting, until the shape of Fearless showed in the doorway. He gave a big satisfied sigh into the night and withdrew inside, and we rose up from the shadow of the paling fence and hedge and started back across the sandhills to the sleeping-hut and the distress signals. We stumbled over pieces of the discarded seaweed armour and found them clammy and losing their elasticity.

We had an inkling of why Teresa liked to do cart-wheels on a Friday.

7 Angelus bells tolling in the chapel, the chink of a nun's Rosary beads as she slipped with beating skirts through the dormitory, cattle and sheep in the saleyards — these were the early morning sounds we knew until we came to Captain's Folly. Now we woke to the screechings of milling seagulls and the sharp dawn shatterings of the waves.

Before breakfast we inspected the Red Indian motorbike by daylight. It was the skeleton of a fighting bull somehow turned into cold steel and fitted with wheels.

"Who'll dare me to sit on it?" Spark said.

"I will," said Maps, normally the one to respond.

We had a fresh impression of the machine's size as Spark had to haul himself up into the seat, and even then it was as if he were perched on the blade of an outsize shovel. He began to show off, leaning forward and just managing to stretch his arms wide enough to grasp the grips on the handlebars. He pinched the black rubber bulb of the horn. It gave a squeak. He swung out of the seat fast and jumped to the ground, and we all bolted for cover in the sandhills, but neither Fearless nor Teresa appeared.

The McAnshes did not rise early that morning, so we started up the valley, at first attracted by some dull wooden hammering from the boat that now lay exposed. No sign of the man building it. He was inside the hull somewhere.

Flower by flower, cluster by cluster, the ice-plant

tapestries were breaking out in the McAnsh front garden and in patches farther up the valley. A tight island of pine trees loomed to one side of us. Beyond them was a patch of lupins with yellow and mauve blooms. Farther up still was another territory that we marked for exploration, the ruins of what had been the main encampment at the time of the Depression.

We poked around in the valley's rubbish-dump, stirring up dust as if reawakening a fire that had been smouldering quietly for perhaps as long as Shellback had been after his groper. Spark began to auction an iron bedstead. We often baited him at St Roderick's by making frivolous bids, but now we joined in his fun, shouting through veils of slowly rising dust, hazarding imaginary fortunes, so much so that had we been persons of wealth that ancient bedstead would have brought the price of an old master.

My find in the rubbish-dump began as a glimpse of faded gilt on carved wood. I took hold of it and tugged, dragging it through a pocket of ashes, and then in my hands I had a small ornate picture-frame.

It was empty, but as soon as I had shaken and brushed it free of ash I filled its four sides. I framed the glassed-in turret-room and the gilded weather-vane above Lady Hodge's mansion. The space was almost square. I could squeeze my face into it, but it was too small to allow my head to go through. I felt I had the prize find by far as we came down the valley, Misty with half a deer's antlers, Maps with some old magazines, Fido dragging a tin canoe, while Spark persisted in trying to auction our finds for us.

Meanwhile, the McAnshes were pathetically subdued. Bandy let out a belch not exactly in keeping with the debonair and gentlemanly character who had been described to us the previous evening. His wife gave him a sharp look. His popularity had slumped overnight. I noticed that he glanced a little sadly towards the empty wine-bottles.

There was still no sign of Fearless as we settled ourselves in the sandhills.

Using the picture-frame, I located Socrates the horse standing motionless and looking out to sea. The wild cats did not show themselves. A seagull turned slowly on an up-draught, almost at a stop, only the tips and back edges of its wings moving. There were watermarks on the sea's surface caused by currents that swirled around the headlands. These marks were like those on the silk linings of the priest's Benediction copes, the most magnificent of the vestments to come from the workrooms at St Roderick's. I was beginning to realise what the sea reminded me of. It was a sort of manifestation of the notion of eternity. It seemed limitless. It might stretch on for ever and ever. My religious upbringing seemed to have instilled a special fear of eternity into me. But perhaps this is only proof that a man's main vanity — his belief in his own immortality — is alive at a very early stage in his life.

The picture-frame was ready to catch at an instant a full-length portrait of Fearless.

8 Our attempts to get Shellback talking had to negotiate some difficult openings. The prod delivered by Misty on our second morning was not one that he appreciated.

"Mister, were you on that sailing ship?"

"Me on what sailin' ship?" Utter astonishment.

"Th' one out there!" said Misty, pointing into the bay.

"Holy hell!"

"You said you were a sailor, mister."

"How old d'ye think I happen t'be?"

Misty treated this question as if it merited a serious answer. "Well, they reckon there's a tortoise still alive that knew Captain Cook."

Shellback showed his two side-teeth — like inverted commas — so that they gave a sort of formality to his speech, as if he might have been quoting from some authorised text. "A little av that sort av cackle will be goin' a long way with me, won't it?"

He seemed relieved, despite having been credited with superhuman longevity, to talk about Fearless. "Yis, as ye've seen for yeselves, he comes hurtlin' back av a Friday night, but on a Saturday mornin' he's a tired man. If there wuz somebody out there drownin' he'd not be cuttin' too many fancy overarm strokes out to his rescue. He's the beltman av the local life-savin' team, ye know, but thin he's fully entitled t'be tired at the end av a week after all the tunnellin' he does."

"What tunnelling?" someone promptly asked.

"He's the head av a whole gang, isn't he?" said Shellback, as though we should have known this, too, without having to be told. "They're workin' on the new underground railway below the city, and it's long shifts an' hard work, though I'm told the pay is commensurate with the effort involved."

"Why are they buildin' it underground?" asked Fido.

"Stupid," said Spark. "There's no room up on top. Ain't that right, Mr O'Leary?"

"I dare say," granted Shellback in a surly way, eyeing Spark with lips closed dubiously. Sister Catherine, our English teacher, would have rebuked him for his bad grammar, and we half expected this man to do it on her behalf.

Fido still could not grasp why any railway needed to go underground. We came from a part of the world where a train could run for a hundred miles and never knock over a lone tree or an ant-hill. We had seen a little of the city, but that was in the grey of early morning and it left us only with an impression of gaunt buildings and hard unlit windows.

Still, this further information gave us something to mull over. Tunnelling sounded like slavery to us. No wonder Fearless rushed back to the sea and the sunshine on the weekends.

When at length we did see him it was our turn to perplex Shellback.

"Crumbs!" whispered Fido as Fearless wheeled the Red Indian motor-bike through the gap in the sandhills. "He's like a bloomin' war memorial."

"A what?" demanded Shellback.

"A war memorial!" said Fido.

"War-haw-haw-memer-or-iall!" sang Spark.

"He's bronzed to be sure, an' mebbe he's up on a pedestal as far as his young wife's concerned, but thit's a divilish thing to be callin' a live man!" Shellback was dryly amused, even if he did not understand, but we all followed what Fido meant. Fearless wore only shorts, and now he had the size, the legs, the shoulders and the biceps of that bronze Adonis who stood in all weathers at the crossroads near St Roderick's, the only coat *he* ever knew a fine layer of red or yellow outback dust.

We did not stay to explain this to Shellback, because Fearless was astride the motor-bike and at a downward jab of his bare foot it started with a blast that drowned the lazy sounds of the bay. As we ran across to the hard sand, he was already on the move, using his feet as outriggers, his toes curled up. He saw us coming and pinched the rubber bulb of the horn into shrill seagull shriekings and gestured to us to hurry.

He was indeed a human counterpart of that war-memorial Adonis. The motor-bike that had dwarfed Spark seemed just the right fit for Fearless. The engine throbbed under him as if a mad drummer might be locked up inside it. We gathered round, fascinated but a little wary.

As we marched from St Roderick's to the main town church, we had often stopped briefly to look up at that bronze hero at the crossroads. He was garbed like a Greek god, yet he held a Great War service rifle at the at-ease position, and his head was thrown back a little so that he smiled constantly and unblinkingly in face of raw sunlight, dust, darkness and, very occasionally, rain. We had wanted to get closer to that face and the smile, and now as Fearless beamed at us — a beam containing enough smile for everyone at St Roderick's — it seemed that we had achieved our aim.

"All aboard!" he said, and even though he may have been speaking at no more than normal volume, it was as if a bronze chest had chimed.

We were too dazed to understand what he meant, so he ordered Spark onto the handlebars, Misty onto the tank, and Maps and Fido joined me on the pillion seat. We stood up with arms around one another and our spare arms around Fearless' neck.

The invisible drummer locked up in the engine went off his head and we clung fiercely as Fearless' soles began to slide over the sand, the throttle opening, and then we were balanced on two wheels and picking up speed, the words THERE IS NO JUSTICE jigging up ahead of us. As the rocks below Shellback's shack loomed closer, Fearless took us on a wide turn down towards the water, increasing the speed and cutting through tongues of disintegrating foam. The sand became streaked and glazed as I looked down. The earth might have been spinning under us. Spark yelled up front on the handlebars. This was hardly the time for an auction: no, he was calling for more speed. Fearless obliged. Our runs along the hard sand became faster, and we cut deeper into the thin water, cleaving it into curved mirrors either side of us, while Shellback stood out on his ledge, his hands on his hips and a mighty glare focused on us — on Henry's behalf, too, no doubt — like some sort of death-ray. The surf club men were sitting on the sand.

We had been taken once to see a native corroboree at the Aboriginal camp on the outskirts of the outback town. The bull-roarer had fascinated us. A piece of wood was whirled around and around on a length of cord, making a weird throbbing sound. Now I felt that we were riding some sort of bull-roarer, until I became aware of another sound, which I linked with the vibration coming through the great neck I was clutching.

We were strangling him!

It seemed so at first. Then I realised that Fearless was laughing wildly at the fearful ecstasy he was putting us through.

After a dozen laps he stopped and the hot fumes swirled around us. "Had enough?" he asked with a half-moon grin.

For me and Misty and Fido it was much more than enough. We jumped off, then began to reel around giddily. Maps stayed clutching Fearless' neck all on his own, and Spark bounced on the handlebars as he urged Fearless to get moving again. Had Misty, Fido and I known what was to be the consequence of something I would overhear on New Year's Eve, no doubt we would have held on somehow to the end.

Instead, we watched from the dry sand. We were agreed on one thing. As a motor-bike rider, Fearless Foley was a master, a champion, a wonder.

9 Further proof of this awaited us in the combined cottage and shop.

We entered it for the first time escorted by Fearless, who invited us in to celebrate our meeting with cakes and cold drinks prepared by Teresa. He started to tell us how an old railway carriage, part of the Western Flyer that ran to our outback town, had been cut in half to make this building, but he stopped to let us take in the array of framed photographs on the walls.

They told us about another wall. There Fearless stood in riding breeches and boots beside a lightweight motor-bike, his arms folded, his grin a lot younger, the great wooden drum of the Wall of Death behind him. Other photographs showed him garlanded with flowers, weighed down with shields and big silver cups. And then there were some that showed him in action, riding at right-angles to gravity inside the drum, his outline blurred as the earth had been beneath us when we rode along the beach on the Red Indian. I started to hear bull-roarers again.

"Now you know what sort of a maniac I am," he said.

"'Ey! You're ridin' no 'ands!"

"I said I was a maniac."

As he laughed at the compliment he had paid himself, Teresa came in and set down two plates of cakes, and then she went into a chanting speech that seemed to have something in common with Spark's auctioneering outbursts: "There he is warming up! Come now, come now, come and see the desperate Fearless Foley in the very execution of the unique exhibition of riding at sixty miles an hour on an upright wall with his two hands locked behind his back! It's true, it's new, it's terrific! You've never lived till you've seen his debonair daredevil defiance of death!"

"Look! Two of yers!"

Yes, there were two riders on the wall.

"The double death race!" cried Teresa. "Up we go! Round we go! Down we go! We cross, we pass, we overtake each other! Fearless Foley and Cyclone Jones pack into this small man-made circular structure all the spectacle and drama of the thrilling chariot contests of the amphitheatres of ancient Rome!"

Someone now seized upon another discovery. "Miss! Is that you?"

Teresa peered at the photograph in question: a slim young woman in riding breeches, boots, open-necked shirt. There was no doubt in our minds. It was her, all right, despite the way she teasingly withheld immediate recognition of herself.

"Yes, I think it is."

"Can you ride a motor-bike?"

"I could once."

"Lookit! No 'ands, no feet!"

This was quite as amazing as any of the pictures of Fearless, because it showed Teresa lying flat on the tank and seat of the speeding motor-bike, her arms outstretched like wings, her feet swooping up behind her, heels together. No wonder she could do cartwheels with such ease.

Fearless took up the spieling now. "We bring you the very ultimate that the human mind is capable of conceiving in defiance of death! A lady rider will perform astonishing acrobatic feats, in which she will assume the posture of a bird in flight, and yet she will still manage to remain in contact with a machine hurtling around this twenty-foot perpendicular wall at sixty deadly miles per hour! Give her a hand, ladies and gentlemen, give her a cheer!''

Fearless cheered and we joined in with him. This whirl of discovery was making me dizzy. My head was becoming that wooden part of a bull-roarer.

''Why'dja give it all up?''

''I had her stopped, that's why,'' explained Fearless.

''Stopped?''

''She was stealing my thunder!''

A soft look passed between him and Teresa, which seemed to be explained some time later when Shellback O'Leary told us that she had suffered an accident. That was all before the travelling show, of which the Wall of Death was part, broke up at Serenity. Fearless and Teresa had come over the hill to Captain's Folly, bringing with them the old-style railway carriage that had been a hut for workmen when the electric line was being laid from the city to Serenity. Cut in half, the two parts were set parallel and joined by a new room. One end was made into the counter for Teresa's small shop, and this became the bay's depot for supplies and mail.

We ate and drank, our eyes still on the framed photographs. No wonder Fearless could hurtle down that zigzag road in the dark.

He must have been watching us for some time before he suddenly spoke his thoughts. ''How is it you chaps haven't been adopted off?''

''Fearless!''

Teresa stood aghast in the doorway to the kitchen. As Fearless realised his blunder, he looked at us sheepishly, the edges of his mouth eager to start up a smile. We were not upset in the least. In fact, he had our sympathy. It

41

was the sort of mistake we ourselves were apt to make. And he smiled with great relief when he saw that we were not offended.

By way of making amends, he said: "I heard a terrific joke the other day . . ."

However, we were puzzled by the reaction from Teresa in the kitchen.

"Oh, Fearless, must you?"

"It's clean. The boys'll love it."

"*If* they ever hear it!"

This puzzled us even more — until he began. Long before he reached the point of the story he was laughing. The harder he tried to get on with it, the more he laughed. His eyes reddened and streamed with water. It was as if by telling a story he brought on a flash attack of some strange allergy. He appeared to be in danger of having convulsions. Teresa came to the doorway and shook her head in mock sadness at the helpless spectacle he was making of himself. We never did hear that story, nor any other story, but the sight of him trying to tell it became a source of hilarity for us, so that we regarded it as a very happy affliction for him to possess.

Later in the day, sated with food, I used the picture-frame to capture some imaginary glimpses of Fearless and Teresa on the Wall of Death. I buried it in the sand-hills and marked the spot with a stick of driftwood. That picture-frame and my imagination were to cause me trouble in the weeks to come.

10 The stern and frugal life at St Roderick's could not help but foster petty enmity among us, but at Captain's Folly it vanished as we entered into a world of sunshine and freedom. I had a divination that heaven

or paradise must be a place where all rivalry and competition — and the causes of them — are banished for ever. We were no longer the same black-hearted altar boys who conducted races after Sunday evening's Benediction with cone-shaped extinguishers, the winner being the one who put out the most candles fastest. No longer did we seem to be the same elbowing urchins fighting over the morning basket of bread and jam because one slice looked thicker than another or was more generously spread with plum- or fig-jam. We were spared the humiliation of having to toady with false politeness to the nuns for a smile.

Our fifth day beside the sea was the last day of December. By this time we were shedding some old skin, although Teresa's sunburn lotion had saved us from any serious injury.

Fearless was due back for the night, but we had the day to put in first and we began it by paying a call on Shellback O'Leary. Among other things he had described how the two halves of the railway carriage were brought down the zigzag on the back of a truck's trailer.

" 'Twas a livin' miracle," he said, "how all thim six bends were negotiated an' the two pieces were brought t'the valley floor instead av tumblin' down into piles av matchwood. If ye look close enough under all the cream paint thit's bin slathered over the two bits, ye'll see thit it wuz the first-class restaurant car. A sorry end, but thin this is a great place fer the dumpin' av past glories." We found that he remained unshakable in his dedication to the belief that the Depression had been a time of harmony among nations and goodwill among men.

He was scornful of our hope that the coming evening would be an occasion. "I'll tell ye what. 'Twill be a miserable sort av an affair be comparison with the festivities thit wunce accompanied th' event here in the

43

valley. There wuz a fella livin' here who constructed his own fireworks. No, I'm tellin' ye no lie. His own fireworks. Great soarin' rockets they were, whole eruptions av stars, together with whirlin' things thit spun around in pursuit av their own fiery tails. It wuz this fella's trade, ye see, but in the days av the Depression there wuz not the demand for such wasteful extravagance, so he came here to the valley to be with the rist av the boys. And no doubt somewhere up there in the deserted remains av the places where they lived there's a store av thim . . ."

A store of fireworks!

"Indade," Shellback insisted. "In fact I've wondered often to meself when there'd be a fire startin' up and runnin' through the long grass until it struck the hidden arsenal to give us the explosions av a New Year's Eve in the middle av a hot summer's day." The prospect of this amused him, but only briefly. "Though it'd happen, I'll be bound, jist when Henry wuz gettin' ready to take a gulp of me baited hook an' so frighten him off."

There would not be any fireworks lingering in that abandoned camp to boost any runaway fire, if we could help it. We left Shellback to drool to his heart's content over those days of mankind's despair, and we passed by way of the gap in the sandhills up to the camp itself.

The shapes of former gardens were visible like untidy darns in some festering fabric. Rhubarb, onions, potatoes and cabbage had gone to seed. We managed to form pictures of the inhabitants of the deserted huts and humpies from what still covered the walls, from newspaper and magazine cuttings, their own drawings and scrawls, and a few curling photographs. In one hut, which contained the remains of two bunks, the occupants had obviously been film fans: the walls were pasted with magazine pictures of Marion Davies, Jean

Harlow and Janet Gaynor. In another hut there must have been sports enthusiasts, for here were pictures of Sir Henry Segrave and his *Golden Arrow*, the golfer Gene Sarazen, the finish of the hundred-metres sprint at the Olympic Games in Los Angeles and Gene Tunney making a knock-out.

In others the occupants had been either politically-minded or simply interested in the news of the day. There were headlines from newspapers with statements by Prime Ministers and black-type guff from world economic authorities analysing the causes of the Depression and promoting their own cures; over some of these were derisive comments in faded ink. Elsewhere, the American explorer Commander Byrd was flying to the South Pole, and an upstart major was riding forward at the opening ceremony of the Sydney Harbour Bridge to cut the ribbon with a sabre. There were lists of figures, possibly from card games, and a calendar three years old.

A few huts had floorboards; others had decaying coverings of canvas, sacking or worn linoleum; but mostly the earth was bare, though with grass growing long and pallid, and in one were stunted lupin bushes bearing a few miserable blooms. We probed these floors and looked under the coverings, but there were no fireworks. Yet the search was not without a reward. One hut gave up a cache of fishing gear, enough bamboo rods to equip us with one each, the cord of the lines unperished and the hooks still sharp, even if rusted.

The area was not completely uninhabited. Firstly, there were what we might have called Fearless-sized daisies: big bright sunflowers growing against peeling walls as if in proof of the dignity and grace of the people who had once lived here. Secondly, there was the ghost.

Maps pointed across to another hut and said: "That

place is haunted." Simply by saying things like this he could jar us. Now there was undeniable evidence for what he claimed: a flubbery groaning sound. Was the Devil here at Captain's Folly? According to Sister Catherine back at St Roderick's, Satan used weird and illogical noises to proclaim his presence. He had been known to linger at the site of an unsolved murder and discharge ten-ton loads of invisible gravel in a great rushing roar against the side of a house. Perhaps in the days of the Depression someone had been murdered here.

"Go on," said Maps to a curious but wary Spark. "I dare you to sneak over and wake him up."

"Wake up who?" countered Spark.

"That ghost. The snorer."

"Awlaright," said Spark, pulling the top of his pants up through his belt and drawling his acceptance, a habit he had of arraying himself on taking up a challenge. "Awlaright, I'll try. Hi-hi!"

It was some years since we'd had first-hand experience with a snorer, a nun who slept in the curtained four-poster in our dormitory. She had snored with a silencer on her beak compared with this ripe performer.

The hut was larger than most, with a tin roof and glassless windows. The rest of us held back as Spark crept across to the corner of the hut, then craned up to one of the window openings and peered inside. Spark was the wild cat going down to pick up one of the fish caught by Socrates the horse, and we were the offspring waiting behind.

Rich and unbroken, the snores continued.

Spark ducked down again and came back to us at a crouching run.

"Whoozit?" Maps demanded.

"Rip Van Winkle."

" 'Oo's 'e?" asked Fido.

"The fella that went to sleep for half a lifetime an' woke up with a long white beard," said Spark. "He was usin' it for bedsocks."

Here was an intriguing possibility. Someone had come here to escape from a city in the grip of hunger, from the misery of its jobless streets and the humiliation of the queues outside the soup-kitchens, only to fall into an unbroken sleep extending into times of relative prosperity.

Suddenly Maps had to cope with a challenge.

"Dare you to wake him up."

"Mightn't want to be woke."

"Why don'cha ask him?" suggested Spark, giving a raw laugh and his private war-cry: "Hurrum! Hoo! Hee! Haw!"

Maps eyed him for a moment then accepted. "I'll take you up," he said, but the coldly suspicious look on his face did not change.

"Tickle his feet," called Spark. "Ick-dick-mick-tickle 'em!"

Now Maps played the part of the wild-cat parent. I know that Misty and Fido shared my envy of the calm way he could take up a challenge.

The snores drifted over to us: strangulated whistlings, rumblings, lips walloping each other. Maps took a swift peep in through the glassless window. He turned to us with the barest shadow of a smirk on his face, making it rather evil, and sauntered back.

To Spark he said: "Hasn't got no feet."

Not only was the snorer a hangover from the good old days of the Depression, but apparently he was also a legless veteran of the Great War.

"Awlaright," said Spark, "pull his tail."

Maps put an end to the mystery by cupping his hands together and bawling: "Happy New Year!"

The snoring stopped, and a grey shape rose above the level of the window-sill, and both Spark and Maps disgorged jeering laughs as the rest of us realised that the ghost was Socrates the horse. Greater power to his big white teeth! Might the coming year find him catching fatter fish and more of them! We accepted this as a cheerful leg-pull. It was a reflection of our joy at being set free in a place like Captain's Folly, a sort of singing.

All too soon, unfortunately, sour notes were to creep into it.

11 As shadow filled the bay, we felt that New Year's Eve was really starting.

The hills behind Captain's Folly blocked out a view of the sun going down, but its farewell banners always reached out over our heads to touch the sea with crimson and lilac. Once, when we saw a passing ship lit up with a deep orange-gold, we knew what a ball of splendour the sinking sun must be.

Fearless arrived an hour or so after darkness had settled, a fighting sabre of light running ahead of him down the zigzag road, the roar of the motor-bike his war-cry. On the turns the beam probed around, very briefly illuminating the words about justice. It churned the simmering blackness as if intent on stirring the night to a thicker consistency. When Fearless took Teresa into his arms, the helmet, leather coat and leggings made him so huge that she seemed to vanish in his embrace.

Bandy McAnsh had been over the hill to Serenity and he and his wife had a bottle of wine. The effect of its contents left us free to wander. We put on our pyjamas and then slipped away from the sleeping-hut to watch the events of the night.

The surf club pavilion was the scene of the party. The doors on its ground floor were open. A keg of beer was set up and tapped. Music came from a portable gramophone. A power line brought electricity from Serenity, and under a shade encrusted with dried salt a globe cast a tent of light out front, reaching almost to where the sandhills rose either side. The waves caught some of this light as they plunged shoreward, and they might have been frenzied cattle and sheep swarming under arc-lamps into the saleyards next to St Roderick's.

Where the light from the globe merged into the dark we scooped shallow trenches and lay waiting for the fun to start. We had little idea of what to expect, but there was plenty of promise in the air.

Fearless had changed into shirt and shorts, and he came down with Teresa on his arm.

"Up we go, down we go, around we go," Spark began to murmur at the sight of them.

The surf club men were all considerably younger than Fearless. They had girls staying with them. Tinny music from the gramophone. Dancing. Fearless in charge of the keg. Shellback arrived — the same dangling shorts, but a white shirt and a tie as broad as the paddle of a canoe. He brought his own pewter pot. His feet were still bare.

"Wait till he starts dancin' around," whispered Spark. "Teresa wants to watch out for her feet."

We openly referred to her by Christian name now, although it was "Miss" to her face.

No need to worry. Shellback was no dancing man. He eyed the scuffing and behind-wiggling with a sort of sullen disapproval.

The McAnshes appeared and went straight into a dance side by side. No ordinary two-step this. They were trying to shake the dry sand out of their shoes without having to take them off. The keg was their first port of call. No sign of the valley's First Lady. We had not sighted her yet, only her housekeeper and a duster of a dog. Also absent was the owner of the grand piano, who we came to know as Fingers Galore. The man with the obsession about justice was referred to locally as Double Martin, and he was not present either. We were to have the honour of nicknaming the man who made the wine, but he was another of those missing.

Tubby Porter was there, the man dedicated to building a boat; he seemed to have chosen this task to prove that it could be done by a man who looked physically unsuited to it. He was fat, bald, purple-faced, triple-bellied, a constant perspirer, a gasper with trembling hands and a trap-door in his throat when it came to swallowing beer. According to the categories of drinkers described to us by Mrs McAnsh, he was the perfect guzzler. Shellback would have been his match tonight, except that he kept yabbering at Fearless. While he changed records and filled mugs with beer, Fearless nodded as if listening. He had large ears: they would take a lot of filling.

At the height of the whirl, one of the surf club men slipped away into the darkness with a girl.

"Off canoodling," said Spark. He did not leave it at that. He went on to endanger our position by recklessly embroidering it. "Can-diddle!-oo-oo!-diddle-diddle!-oodling!"

A desperate whisper from Maps: "Shuddup!"

Just to be witnesses to the party was to savour freedom. We used to lie awake in the dormitory at St Roderick's at the beginning of other New Years.

Throughout the town car-horns had tooted and people had joined in singing "Auld Lang Syne". Here at Captain's Folly we did not know what to expect other than some crescendo at midnight.

A female screech came from the darkness where the man and the girl had gone.

"That's Socrates," said Spark.

"'E don't scream."

"No, the dame screamed, because Socrates kissed her first. Schmoosh-schmoosh-schmoosh!"

Again we had to quieten Spark.

The absence of the couple was of no further concern to us for the moment. Fearless stepped out onto the concrete plaza in front of the building and threw a record, boomerang fashion, into the darkness. We heard it swish like some night bird as it looped over our heads, then the whunk as it dug into the sand. We recovered it and found a copy of "Home on the Range" warped like a badly starched wimple.

Suddenly the man who had gone off lurched back into the pool of light, minus the girl. He waved out to the black maw of the bay. The music stopped as someone lifted the head off the record. The waves brayed. Fearless pulled off his shirt and yelled orders.

One moment the men were dancing, the next they were running into their places as members of a life-saving team. Fearless slipped into the belt lying near the old chariot-type reel that had been casting a spooky shadow across the sand and dashed into the water, taking the line with him, as the chariot reached the wet sand. Three men took their positions on the line and paid it out over their heads as Fearless entered a world of oily ink and frothing whitewash. The impact of his body against the waves made silvery fans of spray. Farther out in the moonless dark the waves were faint serrations. There was no sign of a woman drowning.

Light came from two sources. A car was driven to the gap between the sandhills and its headlamps aimed across the heads of the men on the line, so that a beam provided a path for Fearless as he swam through the breakers. Either side of him now the waves jostled angrily to force their way into the light, frenzied white-faced bullocks. The McAnshes, Shellback, Tubby Porter and some of the men and girls from the party were clustered about the reel. The other light came from the Red Indian motor-bike, pushed up into the sandhills by Teresa and two of the men. The beam was aimed out ahead of Fearless and swung slowly from one side of the bay to the other. A few gulls and petrels dipped and tumbled through it.

We weaved our way through the sandhills to be near the rise where the motor-bike stood. One of the surf club men was trying to reassure Teresa. "We won't lose him," he said. "He's on a strong line."

"That line's no protection against sharks."

"This isn't a shark bay."

"How can you be sure?"

"No one's ever been taken here."

"And I've never known anyone go swimming out like that into pitch blackness. The silly girl!"

At least the beams did not reveal any sharks' fins. But this was the domain of Henry the groper, and he was a man-mauler if not a man-eater. We shared Teresa's ordeal.

Fearless stopped and faced the shore. The Red Indian's headlamp kept sweeping the bay. The sea began to seem a vast grave, the white of the waves the raw material for tombstones. Then someone by the reel shouted and pointed to the northern end of the beach, and the motor-bike's beam was swung there at a depressed angle.

It lit up the missing girl.

She splashed through the shallows in a tipsy walk, naked, laughing, dragging a sodden frock behind her. Her boy friend ran to her and tried to make a shawl of the frock as she flopped into his arms, then took her up through the sandhills to his car. From the water's edge we heard Shellback's voice standing out against the sound of the waves and felt cheated of something pungent when we could not hear his actual comments.

Fearless was hauled ashore, and as he stood on the beach and shook the water out of his shorts it must have been right on the dot of midnight. Through the open front of the abode of the man known as Fingers Galore came a regal rendition of "Auld Lang Syne".

12 The McAnshes started the New Year by helping each other to negotiate the sandhills. We stayed on.

Fearless came back from the shop in a pair of dry shorts, and left it to others now to fill the mugs and change the records. He showed no sign of being put out by the unnecessary and perilous swim. He camped in a deck-chair out on the plaza and Shellback was soon there beside him like a big, angry moth, belting Fearless' ears with chunks of talk. We were not near enough to be able to sort it out into words. They sat between us and the electric globe, and the shadows of the mugs of beer rose and fell towards us, the size of the scoops on giant mechanical shovels. Between swigs both men left their beers on the plaza.

"Anyone ever tasted beer?" someone whispered.

No one was able to claim the distinction.

"Wonder what it's like," mused another.

The night must have made me recklessly lightheaded. Suddenly I found myself issuing a general challenge: "Who'll dare me to find out?"

"I will!"

It was a double-banger of an acceptance, from Maps and Spark, both only too pleased to find someone else prepared to indulge in the dangerous business of dares. The sand squealed in tiny dry discords under the fabric of my pyjamas as I used Fearless' shadow to cover my wriggling approach. His beer sat in this same shadow a few feet from the edge of the concrete plaza which rose sharply into a high step, and this also threw a shadow. I was just within its slant when Shellback jumped onto the edges of his root-like feet. I rolled in beside the plaza, my heart battering. But it was not me he had spotted.

"Look at the cheek av thim, the motherless young divils thit they are!" he cried, while Fearless peered around, just in time to glimpse four midget ghosts scrambling over a sandhill.

"And it's about time, be Gawd!" Shellback shouted after them. "Up out av bed at this hour, ye'll all ind up a pack av pagans, what with nude wimmen runnin' berserk on the beach an' a mad galoot in a cave thumpin' out some Scottish dirge!"

Fearless laughed and told Shellback to sit down.

"I saw it out av the corner of me eye," Shellback explained, as I kept pressing myself close to the concrete edge. "A sort av waverin' whiteness it wuz, an' for a moment I thought it wuz more young wimmen mauraudin' about with their clothes abandoned. Thim two wine-bibbers ought to be keepin' a stricter watch over their charges." He ignored another suggestion from Fearless to sit down, and then went on to put in words what I had felt about the McAnshes. "Av course, they've concocted this holiday business, an' talked her diminted ladyship inta bein' the benefactress, jist so's they might be able to show off what a pious pair they are to all thim sinners thit congregate in the church over in Serenity."

"Shellback, sit down," said Fearless for the third time. "That's better. Whatever their reason, they're not doing those kids any harm. Just think of it. This is the first time they've ever seen the sea in their lives."

"Yis," moped Shellback, again loyal to his obsession. "And whan I think av all the time I've spint tryin' ter catch thit confounded groper, I wish I'd niver set me two eyes upon the sea meself."

"Have a lash at your drink," urged Fearless.

Shellback complied, and behind me a shadow rose, paused and fell.

"What do you reckon about those boys, anyway?" Fearless asked.

"Reckon about thim?"

"Think of them?"

"Why the divil should I be thinkin' av thim? Haven't I got enough on me mind without thinkin' about thim embryo hooligans?"

Fearless chuckled.

"Why the hell should ye ask me a question like that?"

"Teresa keeps talking about them."

"Yis. An' I kin tell ye why. Since this place got abandoned to rack an' ruin, there's bin a disastrous dearth av customers t'keep her busy. The end av the Depression was a terrible ivent for ye, and ye have me sympathy, both av ye." Something caught Shellback's eye at the north of the beach and his shadow fell heavily behind me as he stood up.

Fearless was still tired after his swim. He spoke on without realising that Shellback's attention was elsewhere: "When we got married it didn't seem right to have any children. First there was the sort of life we led with the travelling show. And after her accident — for a long while after it — we were led to believe it'd endanger Teresa's life to have a child. Then came the bad times, and it seemed wrong to bring kids into such a world. I don't know whether we felt strong about this or whether we were swayed by some of your tub-thumping mates. Anyway, now it seems nothing can happen between us. My fault, I suppose, breathing fumes underground all week. Yet when I got home last Friday night, she kept talking about those kids. I've got an idea . . ."

"Yis, indade, Fearless boy, ye're full av ideas, full av bright ideas," said Shellback, but he might have been Bandy McAnsh murmuring one of his distorts.

"I don't reckon on rushing it. Give her a few weeks. Give her time to get to know the kids properly. Then one night I'll say to her: 'Let's make up for lost time. Tell me which of those five boys you like best and we'll adopt him!' What do you reckon about that?"

"It's only thit grey horse moochin' about," said Shellback in place of an answer as his shadow sat down once again. "I had meself startled inta thinkin' it wuz another wimman divestin' herself av clothin'."

"Anyway," said Fearless going on with his side of the conversation, "that's what I intend to do."

"Ye'll do what ye want t'do, Fearless, ye're that sort av a fella. And now I'll git meself another mug av beer."

"Me, too. Besides, it's getting a bit cool out here."

Two great shadows rose this time and withdrew.

As I lay against the concrete, I felt as if some infinitely precious tincture had been dropped into my ears, a glowing globule in each, and that my body had been transformed into a sort of tabernacle to hold a rare secret.

A nasal foxtrot came from the gramophone. The waves fell. I wriggled along the edge of the concrete plaza to the point where the front of the pavilion cut off the electric light, and then scuttled through the sandhills back to the sleeping-hut.

"Anythin' 'appen?" asked a voice on behalf of the seven eyes waiting in the darkness.

"No," I said. "I just had to wait till Fearless an' Shellback went inside."

And so I kept the discovery to myself and began the New Year with a fearful secret.

13 My closest companion in the days that followed was the picture-frame.

My head became numb like a foot going to sleep as I tried to assess the chances of Spark, Maps, Misty and Fido as Teresa's first choice. Only the picture-frame was able to take my mind off this, and I used it as a window and as an ear. I framed patches of sky as deep as eternity and as blue as Fearless' eyes. Once I caught the golden-green of Teresa's eyes near the horizon. Towards sunset one day, the four sides enclosed a patch that seemed to have been spread with slightly wrinkled gold leaf, the sort of sky I had seen in convent prints of early Italian paintings. The ice-plant flared on the burning days and kept its hues muted on the dull. The breeze brought the smells of the beach at low tide to where the frame was set up in the sandhills. A sightseeing launch from the jetty at Serenity cut its engines and drifted, while a man's voice echoed around the bay as he told the passengers how Captain's Folly had come by its name.

There was a rush to the side to try to glimpse the wreck. The launch tipped and the water frowned on that side. The man cried out to the passengers to hold back or the boat might capsize. Yet I could not see this man, and so it was as if the launch itself had spoken. Such was the power of the picture-frame to transform reality.

Just what were my chances against the others?

Teresa had never shown any special interest in me, except to ask why I came to be called Choker. Spark explained that it was because in class at St Roderick's I suffered a tightening of the throat when told to stand up and answer some question. She gave me one of her soft smiles that was always accompanied by a rather musical little sigh of sympathy, and after that at the daily oiling with sunburn lotion she called me Choker as if it were my natural name. At this same oiling, Fido and Misty received the gentlest treatment. Fido because of his size? Misty because he had only one eye? Did that mean I must starve to become as thin as Fido or develop a squint in order to compete with Misty? According to my early assessment, Maps was not the type who would appeal to Teresa. Spark was the danger. Of all of us he was the one to raise a smile from the nuns at St Roderick's. His breezy talk and bent for auctioneering seemed to amuse even the sourest of them.

Thus I was sensitive to every glance and word that Teresa directed to any of the others. I had to bottle up a sort of frenzied helplessness. I had secret knowledge, yet I knew no way of putting it to work for me. Say, for instance, I took to parting my hair and picked a bunch of lupin blooms and delivered them to the shop. Pretty soon there would be an inquisition in the sleeping-hut or in a dip of the sandhills, and the truth would be badgered out of me.

Which one of us did Fearless himself seem to favour?

On the first weekend after the start of the New Year I watched him for signs. It was a weekend full of hammering. Tubby Porter seemed to work non-stop for two days: hollow hammerings, thin tappings, as if he were a cricket capable of varying the strength and volume of his playing. He was almost ready to paint the hull and the boat would probably be launched during our stay. The others were excited about this, but I seemed to have lost the ability to live for the present.

The picture-frame helped me watch Fido launch the tin canoe that he had dragged down from the rubbish dump. It was a sheet of tin pinched together at either end with nails and slats and made waterproof with a sealing of tar. Crude outriggers gave it balance. Spark, Maps and Misty helped him launch it from the rocks in the calm out past the point where the waves started to break. With all four of them on board it rode low in the water. If the sea suddenly decided to swamp it and swallow its four occupants I would be the only one left. This was a heinous notion and I found myself frightened at being capable of thinking it. Yet the wish that the others were dead kept recurring more and more as I resorted increasingly to seeing the world through the faded gilt portals of the picture-frame.

14 "Bless me, Father, for I have sinned . . ."
So it began in the confessional.

Another week had passed, and on the Sunday morning the McAnshes led us over the hill and south to Serenity to be in time to tell our sins to Father Scully before the start of Mass. Thus I received my brief to share the secret with the others.

Such sharing involved a public confession, and

throughout the drone of the Mass I pondered hopelessly on how to go about it. The service came to an end with the congregation growling the responses to three special Hail Marys for the missionaries trapped in darkest Manchuria, but I still had no plan.

The McAnshes left us to escort ourselves back to Captain's Folly. They said they had friends to see, but from a high spy-point we observed them making their way by a back entrance to the Dog's Hind Leg, a seafront pub near the one where Mrs McAnsh had fallen for Bandy. I humped my burden over the hill as Spark cheerfully auctioned his way. My problem grew in size through the afternoon. By the time night had fallen and we were in pyjamas and under our distress signals, I was inclined to the opinion that violent murder and big-scale bank robbery had never received a harsher penance.

In the sleeping-hut, as moonlight came in through the open doorway, someone said he could smell the paint from the hull of Tubby Porter's boat. This led to some talk about the boat. It was a way of indulging in the luxury of being able to yarn after lights out, something not allowed at St Roderick's. How was Tubby Porter going to get that whale of a boat down to the water? No one had the answer to this; but suddenly Spark had a different question altogether, and it brought me face to face with my problem so swiftly that I felt I had been winded by a punch under the ribs.

"Hey, listen, Choker, you were a dickens of a long time in at Confession, weren'cha?"

"Yeah! 'E sure was!"

"Whatcha been up to on the quiet?"

They were all at me.

The distress signals, despite their varied daytime colours, were now patterns of grey and black, and the legs and bodies that had made them flutter in the gloom became still as I made my second confession of the day. I told them what I had overheard when I was trapped alongside the plaza of the surf club pavilion after that hectic midnight. They all understood why I had to pass on the information. To hold back would have turned my small and unintentional sin into sacrilege and I would be first stop hell should judgment overtake me. I was conscious that their claws were coming out there in the corners. Their minds would already be racing over the past, as mine had done, recalling every incident involving Teresa, every word or smile or glance from her, in order to assess their own chances. I had been going through this for ten days or so, and therefore I knew what was happening.

No one spoke after I had finished. The dry wiring of the mattresses creaked a little, and then there was only the sound of the sea and a silent turmoil to fill the hut.

We were all remnants of a sort. From the time we had left the nursery section of St Roderick's we could recall other companions being checked out to start new lives. It was not a time when there was a rush to adopt children. We were five who had not managed to take the fancy of any of the prospective parents in the visitors' room, but now each of us had a chance.

The nuns had told us that we could expect to meet up with our parents in the hereafter. In the meantime I am sure we all wondered about them. I still do, and however important or exciting we might have believed our parents to have been, it is certain that we could not have imagined any two people more suitable for the roles than Teresa and Fearless. And so that third role, Teresa's choice, became the most tantalising prize by far ever to be dangled in front of our nine eyes.

15 As befitted the shady roles we were now to play against one another, our skins had become as dusky brown as seaweed. Our bathing-costumes had faded to the grey of stale sea-foam, and the brand marks stood out plainly, a big rooster crowing over the words *Excelsior Flour*. The fabric had stretched so much that we had to tie permanent knots in the shoulder-straps to keep the crutches from catching between our knees.

No one questioned the absolute truth of my account of what I had overheard between Fearless and Shellback O'Leary. We all had grounds for thinking that Fearless might have something like this in mind. When he first introduced us to the photographs that gave us such a vivid picture of the life he had once led, he had asked us rather gauchely why we had not been adopted. And then Teresa's niece had come to stay overnight, a girl our age, yellow hair, tanned limbs, white shorts, orange blouse, shrill seagull voice.

"Fearless says he wants to adopt me," she had boasted.

"Is he gonna?" someone asked.

"Can you imagine my mother and father standing for anything like that!" was the tart answer.

We could imagine her parents being only too happy to allow this, although we could not believe that Fearless would care to be landed with her. She was bossy enough to qualify for an immediate habit and wimple at St Roderick's.

And so, on the morning after my second confession, we eyed one another guardedly at breakfast. We carried out our rostered duties around the McAnsh establishment, and then stepped out into the day. Misty detached himself near the sandhills, leaving four of us to wander down to the rocks to view the morning efforts of the inlet's two most dedicated fishermen — Shellback

O'Leary and Socrates the horse. Shellback seemed content to dangle a baited hook listlessly into the water. Socrates splashed around and snapped left and right at the silver-grey splinters arrowing through the shallows.

We had not yet entered into the business of constantly counting heads and so checking on the whereabouts of one another, but eventually we began to wonder what Misty might be doing on his own.

He was located bobbing about in Teresa's front garden.

Shellback could have hooked the elusive Henry, but we would not have stayed to witness him landing the fish. We scrambled down from the rocks and zoomed across the sandhills, leaving four fresh sets of footprints where the night's dew had dried out into a fragile crusting.

Maps slowed to a saunter, allowing three of us to run ahead and range ourselves along the paling fence and low hedge to take in the spectacle of the quiet Misty Hayward plucking out weeds and green shoots.

What was he up to? Trying to follow in Bandy McAnsh's pigeon-toed footsteps and call himself a gardener?

Misty had developed a mannerism for use when he wanted to make a point of ignoring anyone. He closed his good eye almost completely and faced his audience with the opaque pane. And he did this now to the rest of us, and then put his head down again and continued with the weeding as if he had not seen us.

"Whatcha think ya doin'?" came an outraged demand.

Misty weeded on. From inside the cottage came the sound of a tune from the battery wireless. Teresa sang a few lines.

"Is she payin' you?"

" 'Ow much?''

"Careful ya don't go rootin' up good flowers.''

It seemed that Misty's ears as well as his right eye were now out of action. Teresa came to the doorway and we ducked down and watched through the bush and the paling fence, and no doubt all winced at the fond smile she gave the flying starter, Misty. She withdrew inside, and our tangled fringes and cowlicks rose up again.

"Buzz off!'' hissed Misty.

He grabbed up a clod and prepared to throw it. We were ready to duck again.

"Buzz off!'' he repeated.

"Go on, tell us. How mucha gettin'?''

"Nothin'.'' He was desperate.

"Whatcha doin' it for then?''

"Buzz off!''

The clod flew, but we were down in time and it passed well clear of any head.

"I know what's happened,'' said Spark, first up again. "You offered. You offered to do this weedin'.''

We all remembered Teresa saying that she must get around to some weeding. Misty became more threatening and we knew that Spark had guessed correctly. "Look, clear out! Hop it, the lotta ya!'' He threw a second clod, this one aimed at Spark, who again dodged down safely, to pop up with: "I reckon I ought to give you some help.''

Despite more clods and hissed threats, Misty found himself sharing the weeding. Not only with Spark. Fido and I also joined in. We started to snatch out anything that looked like a weed. The scrambling had attracted Teresa's attention over the sound of her wireless and she came out, gaping at our furious industry.

"Blow me down!'' she cried, borrowing one of

Fearless' expressions. "What goes on here? Have you kids started up a local branch of the Boy Scouts?"

"Going! Going! Gone!" cried Spark, accounting for three separate weeds in quick succession.

Misty was entitled to tell Teresa the truth of what was happening, but how could he? That would be a very bad move. To show any hostility to the rest of us — especially when we were volunteering ourselves — would hardly commend him in Teresa's eyes.

"Steady on a tick," she said, and that was another expression we had heard from Fearless when he was drilling the surf team. "This must be my lucky day. If you're really so anxious to help, I'm only too happy to benefit."

The upshot. Spark: the mower and the small lawn at the back. Fido: rags, a tin of polish, ash-trays and the big brass cartridge case that Fearless had brought back from Europe at the end of the Great War. Me: more rags, bucket, ladder and the front windows.

What about Maps? After being so mysteriously reticent he strolled over. He did not give Teresa a chance to think up a job for him. "Excuse me, Miss," he began, "Would you be able to spare the time to give me a lesson?"

"A lesson? Now what kind of lesson could I give anyone?"

Maps spun his finger in a circle. "Show me how ta do one of them," he said. "A cartwheel."

This was piracy, treachery, the height of cheek and cunning, and four of us stood shocked. It brought a startled gasp from Teresa, and so it should. Surely she would waste little time putting this two-legged fox in his proper place? To our amazement, however, it seemed that she was considering it. She looked down at what she was wearing, a sun-suit with shorts and top. "Why not?'' she answered, after only a short consideration. ''One good turn deserves another, doesn't it?''

Whose good turn?

No one had a chance to ask this as Teresa went off with Maps to the hard sand. I tried to take my mind off his outrageous stroke by concentrating on my job, but Teresa's copperplate cartwheels and Maps Prior's ludicrous flops and somersaults were reflected through the gap in the sandhills on the window-pane. I sploshed the picture with water, but the rippling effect only made it all the more taunting.

As Maps' coarse hollers reached our ears, we were allied against him. This was the beginning of a shift and switch of alliances: four against one, three against two, all against all, although there were to be times when the five of us were to be forced to take joint action to combat a general threat.

Such seemed to be the result of my having done the penance imposed by the Reverend Father Scully.

16 The picture-frame now became a spy-hole from which I kept watch on the others.

We all found ourselves committed to such a vigilance, constantly counting heads and then investigating should anyone be missing. The free flow of jibe and quip, the unpremeditated exclamations and exultations that had accompanied us in our first two weeks of discovery in and around Captain's Folly now came to an end. We became a broody lot, barbed with suspicion, our eyes furtive, the urge to kick and trample re-awakened in our feet. ''Share the secret with them, my son. The good things of life, and the burdens, are all the better if they are shared.'' I wondered about that. The good priest, like the sea captain drowned long ago, seemed to be guilty of some disastrous folly.

At last I was getting some meaning from that legend picked out in shell in the nearby garden. So far we had not been within listening distance of the man who lived in the cottage above these words. We had seen him every few days, either crossing to the shop to pick up stores and mail, or making his way alone up the valley to the island of pines, where he disappeared for short periods. He would come out with his head bent forward, his hands clasped behind his back, as if he had just undergone some sad experience.

The reason behind his visits to the island of pines became increasingly intriguing, and when Maps decided to go there and lie in wait he had no chance of doing this on his own.

We waited several times, but the man did not leave his cottage. The days were calm, as most days had been since our arrival, but here there was a hushing sound that rose and ebbed, as if an invisible extension of the sea was running through the tops of the trees. We walked over a bared mattress of dry pine needles, disconcerting for a start because of its lack of noise after the squealings that had accompanied us across the soft sand.

Eventually we caught him. His name was Martin Martin. We had gathered this from spotting a letter addressed to him on Teresa's counter, and it explained why he was known as Double Martin. Men to us were either young or old. This man seemed very old and very frail. He stumbled and nearly fell as he passed from the full daylight glare to the shadow created by layers of criss-crossing branches encrusted with live pine needles. We were out of sight, high above him, near the source of the trees' whisperings, hugging the trunks, moulding ourselves into them. The top of the old man's head was a polished dome like that on the marble bust of the deceased benefactor in the hallway at St Roderick's, and evenly fringed with white hair. He had small rimless spectacles clipped onto the bridge of his nose and attached to the buttonhole of a black summer coat by a dark lanyard. On his feet, despite the heat of summer, were bulky carpet slippers chequered red-and-green. He shuffled until he was ringed by the trunks of the pines, and his hands continued to shake as he clasped them behind his back, as if they were agitated by a weak current passing between them. He lifted his head a little and his spectacles glinted weakly in the remains of a beam of sunlight that had managed to penetrate the loose but deep weave of the branches. He suffered from a great hesitation and I was suddenly afraid that by lying secretly in wait we might pay for our curiosity by being witness to something that would terrify or shock us, not through any horror, rather by a sadness. Here below us was surely a ludicrously timid man to be proclaiming to the world in big white letters that there was no such thing as justice.

He coughed, and I twitched and hugged the tree trunk even tighter.

"Ladies and gentlemen," he began, and at that moment it seemed he must be aware that someone was above him in the trees; but, as we were soon to see, he was simply talking to the pine trees, going back to the first move in an event that had plunged him into a state of gentle madness, perhaps hoping that the flow of inarticulated hushings from the trees might shape themselves into a few comforting words of wild arboreal wisdom and so release him from his Purgatory.

As he spoke in his light silver-grey voice, we gathered that he had stood as mayor of the town across the hill.

He seemed to be reciting something he had written out in full and learned by heart, and he kept running himself short of breath. We could not claim to be expert judges of public speakers, but we had been obliged to sit out the fulminations of some fire-breathing preachers, and suffer the threats of other fire-eaters in the form of nuns and Reverend Mothers, so that compared to theirs his speech was pathetic stuff. Our eyes met through the branches and the fringes of dark green pine needles as the man rambled on. For the moment, despite our obsessions with securing the sole patronage of Teresa, we were drawn together by a common interest.

He spoke for ten minutes or so, and then his hands flopped at his side. He looked around slowly, but there was no sign to comfort him, no word, and he shuffled away in his carpet slippers, out into the sunlight, where the sound of the real sea grew louder upon his ears as he made his way back to his cottage.

Down we came out of the trees, using the branches as rungs, and then we made for the most obvious source of information in Captain's Folly.

17 Shellback O'Leary had become a sort of rubbish-dump in human form. Probe him and anything might show up. We usually started with an inquiry about Henry the groper, and he would be off in full spatter, wetting his lips furiously. It was as if he were damping them with nitro-glycerine, so that as soon as he brought them together they were thrust apart again explosively.

"Before God an' the holy saints I swear thit I missed hookin' the artful schwine be the thickness av a thin whisker!" Or: "I'm preparin' a new bait. Potent. 'Twill

be no time, be well assured, before ye'll see him stretched out here on the rocks ready t'be measured an'
discovered for what he is — a true giant amongst giant
gropers." Or more often: "How in the name av Satan's
black heart kin a man be expected t'conduct a mortal
struggle, sich as it surely is, whan thit lunatic across the
bay keeps beltin' out all thit torture? He's warnin'
Henry, what is more. He is, I tell ye. Warnin' him. He's
usin' the compositions av the great Rachmaninoff
t'warn the fish thit I'm after capturin' him."

What bewildered us was the way he mixed threat and
affection, compliment and abuse, in referring to the
groper. Now, when we asked him about Double Martin,
he nodded his head and said: "Haha, so ye've been on
to the track av that unfortunate individual, have ye
now? In due course, no doubt, there'll be no secret in
this place thit's not common knowledge to the lot av
ye."

He gave us another glimpse of his isolated teeth and a
smirk of disdain, and I thought that was all we were to
hear, but he pressed on obligingly. "Frind Martin was
mindin' his own business sellin' newspapers, books,
pens, pencils an' the like, when two conspirin' citizens av
the town approached him with the proposal thit he
should stand for mayor. They would sponsor him, give
him the necessary support. It wuz tantamount to askin'
me, for instance, to stand as a Protestant parson, but
Martin wuz a simple soul. He claimed thit his aptitude
for public speakin' was negligible, but he wuz urged to
forget that, and for the sake av practice why not take
himself to some lonely spot where there wuz nothin' but
trees, and there try out his campaign speech-makin'?
'Talk to the trees,' they said. 'Tis advice thit's been
given to manny an untried person seekin' public office.

"So Martin agrees, he talks to the trees, an' in due

course, in spite av his simple-minded proposals, he's elected an' installed. Ah, but now comes the reckonin'. His two ardent supporters reveal thimselves as being acutely interested in securin' the contract to build the sewerage system thit wuz to embrace the whole town, the same thit put the nightmen out av their jobs an' consigned their cart to the yard for unwanted vehicles. Martin made a great protest, an' then these two schemin' sponsors revealed thit they knew about a certain minor lapse av character in Martin's younger days. Either he cast his vote to give them the contract or his lapse would be made public.

"Martin complied, but it all came out, an' he wuz he in disgrace. Gone wuz his chance of ever makin' anythin' av the dreams he related to the trees. I laughed meself puce when first I heard av it, but I'm sorry for the little man. The shock av it turned his head. There are times when he's not so silly as ye might expect, an 'tis thin he's in a fury writin' letters to the powers av the land, seekin' justice. Most av the time, however, he's no better than an infant, still thinkin' he's makin' his first speech to the trees. That's his story, an' a sorry wun it is, and now if ye'll pay me the honour av ye attention a little longer I'll show ye the bait thit will finally catch the groper."

If smell was any guarantee, it was a deadly bait. It was the flesh of a large shellfish soaked in vinegar. According to Shellback it would prove irresistible to Henry, like snails and frogs' legs to the French, garlic and birds' nests to the Chinese. However, our minds were still dwelling on the bait that Double Martin had taken — and the consequences.

We rarely went near that island of pines again, and we slipped away once when someone yelled from a tree-top that Double Martin was coming. Just to overhear that sorry speech again might somehow involve us in a similar disaster. We should have been warned by this not to monkey around with our destinies.

A truck from over the hill in Serenity started down the zigzag, raising a curtain of pale yellow dust. Was that driver trying to do on four wheels what Fearless accomplished so successfully on two?

"Another confounded lunatic!" muttered Shellback. "He's bringin' the mid-week mail with him, an' if he persists with his high-speed antics I'll be fishin' me pension money out av the deep blue sea. He'll be over thit cliff if he persists in tryin' to emulate the feats av Fearless Foley. An', if it comes t'that, even Fearless himself is capable av goin' too far on wun av thim bends an' hurtlin' out into the breakers along with his Red Indian motor-bike . . ."

All rivalry was put aside. We were instantly united against a common threat. If Fearless plunged into the sea with the heavy coat, leggings and pack to weigh him down, how would any one of us be adopted?

We left Shellback to dab his purple lips with explosive saliva. We stopped in the sandhills and looked up to the zigzag road. There were many points where Fearless might easily go over.

Maps spoke all our thoughts: "We've gotta slow him down."

18 Before we could deal with this peril to Fearless, Teresa posed a problem.

It began one afternoon as we lay submerged in a shallow lake of soft green shade. We were out of sight in the wild lupins opposite the island of pines. This lake defied the laws of free-flowing water and lay slightly up the hillside from the valley floor. The yellow blooms and the mauve jostled on the surface as we fidgeted in the sweetly-scented cool below. Dancing blooms marked our whereabouts.

A clear call brought a quick calm.

"Hey there, you kids!"

As we surfaced, our heads broke through waves of gentle greenery, the petals of the blooms nuzzling our ears with tiny pug-noses.

Teresa waved to us from the edge of the breast-high lupins, where she stood. She had a bag of light khaki material over one shoulder and she was using both hands to strip pokers of lupins of their petals. These she dropped into the bag.

"Who's for a lupin-chase?" she asked.

We waded across to her through the greenery and blooms. She told us that it was a version of a paper-chase and that she had played it with some of the earlier guests of the McAnshes. She patted me and Misty on the head because we were nearest to her, and then she said that we would help her lay the trail. Spark, Maps and Fido would give us a start and then try to catch up with us.

First the bag had to be filled with petals. We all helped. The lupin perfume grew richer and richer; today if ever I get a whiff of it I am back there starting out with Teresa and Misty. The other three were put on their honour to lie below the surface of the lupins and not to peer out until Teresa gave them the signal to take up the chase.

That signal intrigued us. Teresa tucked in her bottom lip. The tip of her tongue showed. She blew, and a piercing whistle hit our ears and echoed around the valley and set that dog yapping behind the walls of Lady Hodge's garden.

"It's easy when you have the knack," she said,

laughing. "That'll be the signal to start, but don't you go telling Fearless about it."

"Why not?"

"Oh, I don't think he likes it. Not that he ever *says* he doesn't approve, but I've a feeling he *thinks* it unladylike. It isn't that he's prim, just shy about things like that, I suppose."

She stripped a final lupin poker and threw the petals at the three chosen to do the chasing. "Go on! Hide!"

And so Spark, Maps and Fido crept away into the lupins, and the blooms on the surface settled as Teresa, Misty and I started out.

Every dozen strides, Teresa let a few crushed petals trickle from her hand, and they shone like clusters of tiny flowers in the dry summer grass. We jogged along at an easy run past the tumbledown camp once occupied by the unemployed, then up the southern hillside, puffing behind the garden of Mr Watson the amateur wine-maker. We glimpsed him standing among tomato plants that were hung with big green and red berries as if still decked out with Christmas decorations. He was wearing a jungle-style pith helmet, and his beard hung from his face like a swarm of smoky bees.

When we reached the top of the hill we sighted another local inhabitant, this one mounted on a horse. He was the man who rented the land from the Government and ran sheep on it.

"I'll bet he thinks we're up to no good," said Teresa with a mischievous smile. "Every once in a while the boys in the valley used to dine off one of his sheep, or so the story goes."

Suspicion emanated from this man and he watched us until a hump of hill rose between us like a permanent swell transferred from the sea. Soon after this Teresa stopped to give the signal. The whistle reached down into the valley, but we could not see the lake of lupins or the other three starting the chase.

We laid many false trails, branch lines that led nowhere, all designed to delay and frustrate the others. We sighted on a nearby headland the mast and abandoned buildings of the signal station that had supplied so much linen to the McAnsh household. We wove around rocks solidly implanted in the clay, and on a narrow sheep-track I was amazed to find several gaunt, empty-eyed faces staring at me, their foreheads and cheeks partly weathered away.

"One of the men from the valley did that," Teresa explained. "He was a stonesman, but in those days people didn't seem to be able to afford elaborate headstones for graves. Duck down quickly, there they are!"

Spark, Maps and Fido were only just starting up the hillside. We were a long way ahead, but we kept on down the hill now until we were a short distance from the beach itself. Here we had our first rest, satisfied that the others would never catch up. The waves were piercingly white, the intensity of this whiteness vaguely matching the pungency of the lupin perfume. Under the water, the rocks showed as dark shadows, one of them the wrecked sailing ship.

"How do the nuns treat you at St Roderick's?" asked Teresa without any lead-up, without any indication why she should ask such a question.

Misty's spectacle panes flashed towards me, and I decided to be benevolent. "Not bad," I said.

"It must be a wonderful life for them."

"Crumbs!" squeaked Misty. "Wonderful?"

"They haven't any worries."

"Gosh, they're always worried. Eh, Choker?"

With a quick nod, I agreed.

"What about, for goodness' sake?" Teresa was asking.

"I dunno, they're always praying," said Misty.

"That wouldn't worry me," she said. Rising, she lifted the khaki bag and started on the last short lap, emptying out the remaining petals.

She casually dismissed the matter, but its effect on Misty and me was much the same as that achieved by Shellback when he had suggested that Fearless might misjudge one of his Friday night arrivals and end up in the ocean.

We slithered down to the sandhills behind her, and then took cover and waited for the others. As they came to the last cluster of lupin petals, Teresa whispered to Misty and me and we jumped up and jeered and cried out that we were the winners, and by the loose rules of the game this seemed to be so.

The next day I managed to slip away alone to pick up the start of that trail of petals. I planned to follow it, and so recapture something of what had involved me so closely in Teresa's presence the day before, but the petals had lost their brightness and perfume. They had shrivelled away to brown smears in the grass, and I did not go farther.

Meanwhile Teresa's interest in the life of the nuns had us all disturbed.

"Is she thinkin' about enterin' a convent?" Fido had asked as we were left together after the lupin-chase, his face too small for all the concern it had to carry.

"She didn't say that," said Misty.

"If she does enter," observed Spark, still trying to assert his masculinity even by outward disdain for Teresa, "she'll end up as cranky as the rest of them."

"They don't get enough sleep," said Maps. "That's their trouble. They're up half the night praying."

Fido said: "I reckon it's all them 'eavy 'abits they wear that's the trouble."

"They've got bad habits, that's what!" cried Spark with a whoop in honour of a venerable pun. "Tot-tot!"

"That ninety-year-old retired Reverend Mother musta done a terrible lot of prayin' in her time," said Misty, on a slight tangent. "Them big Rosary beads she's got around her middle are worn down like old doorsteps."

It seemed there was a chance that Teresa might end up like this, and that, in our eyes, would be an awful waste and also a dismal end to our hopes.

No one suggested what might be done to forestall her, but after our swimming lesson the next day, as we were drying off on the hot sand, Maps started up. He really startled Teresa, so much so that it was obvious she did not have any recollection of what she had said to Misty and me.

"Miss, do you know what happens to the nuns when they get into a convent?" She looked at him quickly, and he spoke on after a very brief pause. "They've gotta have all their hair shaved off."

"Shaved off?" she cried. She had been clutching her knees as she sat, but now her hands went to her hair on either side of her face.

"All of it," Maps emphasised solemnly.

"Why, for goodness' sake?" she asked.

"It's part of the rules," he said. He depended on us for nods of agreement as he put forward evidence. First he told her how, when we were smaller, a nun always slept in the middle of the dormitory. She was installed in what was — in Fido's terms — a thundering four-poster, on a raised platform, heavily shrouded in white curtains. One night Misty had a nightmare, and the nun came out in a long white night-gown and a small cap of the same material. And if that was not enough to convince Teresa, there was the hot night when many of us were wakened by a young woman laughing drunkenly as she wavered along the top of the outside walls, her skirts held up around her waist. We were ordered back from the window, and the nun who had poked her head through the curtains around that big bed had her hair closely cropped like a boy.

By this time the rest of us were adding our comments, and Teresa was watching us warily.

"They've gotta get married, too," put in Spark.

"The nuns have got to get married?" questioned Teresa very slowly.

"Yeah," Spark answered. "They're brides of Christ. They all wear weddin' rings. We ought to know," he went on feelingly, and several of us understood why. "Sister Alphonsus lost hers down the plug-hole, and we had to spend hours digging up a smelly old drain and searching through all the muck."

Teresa eyed him for some moment in wonder, and then she burst out laughing.

"It's a horrible life," said Maps.

"That's not the sort of life I'd like a bit," she said, to our all-round relief. "Besides, I'm married already." She held up her left hand and the small gold ring gleamed in the sunlight.

So much for that danger.

19 Slow down Fearless?
We might just as well expect Shellback to land Henry the groper by beckoning him out of the water

with a fragment of tortoiseshell stuck on the end of a gnarled finger. Yet when Fearless arrived in his usual style the following Friday night, we were more conscious than ever of the risk he took. We found ourselves very much in agreement that for our common interest he must be protected against himself.

The answer came that night when Maps began to think aloud. "Go slow," he said. Then he went on to erect a string of verbal road signs in the darkness. "Dangerous Bend! Deadly Bend! Speed Limit Five Miles an Hour! Loose Gravel! Dangerous Deadly Hairpin Bend!"

The rest of us began to catch on and repeat what he said, throwing in suggestions. Spark's shout topped all others: "BEWARE, MAD ROAD!"

"Boys, boys!" Mrs McAnsh called. "Off to sleep!"

She and Bandy were having a dry night. We were satisfied to obey. We felt we had the answer. The impossible would be achieved. We would slow Fearless down on the coming Friday night.

The next morning we found Captain's Folly invaded by a warm drizzly mist. The ice-plant tapestries barely showed their colour all that day. The headlands were ghostly, and Mr Watson's house and Lady Hodge's mansion were blurred by the damp. It put a surface of grime on everything we handled in the rubbish-dump as we sorted out pieces of board and poles to carry our road signs. We peeled off skins as thick as hippopotamus hide from tins of tar to reveal the sharp-smelling, viscious liquid below, just at the right consistency to use as black fingerpaint. First we planned to make use of some of the whitewash in buckets at the rear of the McAnsh cottage so that we would have sharp backgrounds for the words. I was in charge of the lettering, as drawing was one of my best subjects at St

Roderick's. Indeed, I have warm memories of this talent, having been awarded six cuts from the Reverend Mother's strap across the seat of my pyjamas for drawing speeding racing-cars and motor-bikes on the glossy backs of all the illustrations of the Mass in my Prayer Book.

Some extravagant signs were suggested, but we settled for those that were simple and blunt. A big GO SLOW for the top of the hill, and then others to warn of dangerous bends and patches of loose gravel, a collection of jaunty signs with tumbledown lettering, the whitewash marked and smeared by tarred thumbs and fingers. We secured the flats to the uprights with old nails salvaged from the packing-cases and banana-boxes that had once served around the hovels of the abandoned camp as household furniture, and we used a heavy spanner as a hammer. The job was completed before we realised that it might have been easier to scavenge for nails under Tubby Porter's boat, and perhaps borrow a hammer and some paint.

Another of the nuns at St Roderick's, Sister Ignatius, who was always prepared to talk about the Great War — so much so that I was inclined to believe that she had been thwarted by her sex from being a soldier — had told us about a truce when the opposing sides called off the bayoneting and shooting while they mixed in no-man's-land to sort out and bury their dead. That was us as we worked side by side, cheerfully enough. Yet we were only observing niceties long part of everyday shoulder-rubbing in circles more adult and august than ours. Once the job in hand was over we would be at one another's throats again.

The finished signs were stacked to dry in the hut where Socrates the horse had tricked some of us into thinking that it had given shelter to a Rip Van Winkle left over from the days of the Depression.

"D'ya reckon it'll work?" asked Spark loudly.

The rest of us spun around to find out whom he might be addressing. None other than one of the sunflowers.

"Reckon it'll do the trick?"

The sunflower's head flopped about, thanks of course, to the way Spark shook the stalk. He took its lolling nods as an affirmative answer.

There was another problem to deal with now, one that called for joint policy and united action. There was nothing to stop us going ahead and erecting the signs. We had found spades and grubbers in the abandoned camp among a pile of gardening tools, and we had chosen the spots where the signs were to stand. However, if they went up too early someone might haul them down. The most suitable time to erect them was after sunset on the Friday evening, shortly before Fearless' arrival. This was all very well in theory, but how could we be sure of being free to slip out under the noses of Mrs McAnsh and her beloved Bandy? If it was a dry night for them, they would probably make certain that we were under our distress signals at a time proper for growing boys. On the other hand, if they had a bottle of wine to consume . . .

Maps solved this one for us, too, but not until the Thursday night.

"Lissen, muggins," he said, confronting Spark with another challenge in the sleeping-hut and making it insultingly provocative, "do you remember where old Watson keeps his pumpkin wine?"

Naturally Spark knew, we all knew: on shelves in the shed at the back of his house. Mr Watson had called us over one day as we were returning from an expedition to the top of the hill, where we had marked the occasion by carving our initials with pocket-knives in the foreheads, cheeks and chins of the clay faces. We had gone to the gate in his front hedge, and he had led us around to the shed, handed us a bottle of the pumpkin wine and asked us if we would be good enough to present it to the McAnshes together with his very best compliments.

"I'll tell you what," Maps went on, "I'll dare you to sneak up there and swipe a bottle of that muck an' then give it to Bandy an' his missus. Say that Mr Watson sent it down, like he did the other time, with his compliments. He's half-barmy, so he won't notice it's gone. Go on, I dare ya!"

Spark did not keep us long in suspense. "Awlaright," he said. Then he laughed. "Tell *you* what, I'll make it two. I'll swipe two whole bottles. Two-diddle-doo!"

No doubt we all allayed our consciences with the same argument. What was a bottle or two of that wine to the old man? In any case, we were taking it only to protect Fearless Foley against himself, against his death by drowning, and that surely justified us.

The deed was done the next morning.

To ensure Spark a clear run at the back, the rest of us stood along the front hedge, peered over into the garden and loudly voiced our interest in the sundial. Watson obliged by coming out and inviting us right into the garden. Now we discovered that it was a most unusual sundial. Its markings were not of our hemisphere. They were cut into marble that seemed to be streaked with rust, as a cinnamon loaf is marked with the brown spice that gives it flavour. Across this a thin shadow fell from the slanted bronze finger and we read that it was four a.m. But that was the time in Naples, and there it was apparently a bleak, black four o'clock on a winter's morning.

This was the man we were to treat to the nickname of Sundial Watson, and as he explained his timepiece to us and conveyed a mysterious nostalgia for other times and places, we saw Spark nip across to the shed. We were then informed that if we were to call upon the services of the incomparable Mr Foley and tunnel through the earth from this point we would come out in the middle of the crater of Vesuvius. That was not a very welcome notion at that moment, since we seemed to be hazarding quite enough hell-fire without clawing up through a live volcano.

We were polite listeners until we saw Spark swaying at a jog down the hillside, his balance thrown out by something bulky in the front of the shirt that he had worn for the occasion.

About the time a wintry dawn was breaking over the city of Naples on the other side of the world, Captain's Folly was filled with a carmine mixture of sunset and shadow, and the McAnshes were happily disposing of liquid sunshine in the form of Sundial Watson's pumpkin wine. They had already emptied the first bottle when Spark made the first move to leave.

The McAnshes were not aware of his going. And so we drifted out one by one and headed for the abandoned camp, where we picked up the notices and carried them to various points up the zigzag road. We started putting them in position from the top with the big GO SLOW near the seat at the bus-stop, and then we worked our way down. That first sign, we felt sure, would catch the beam of the Red Indian's headlamp and hit Fearless bang between the goggles. We stamped with the hardened soles of our bare feet until the earth was well tamped around the upright, and then we went down to the next hole. By the time we reached the bottom of the zigzag, the moon was showing up fitfully in a sky strewn with ragged cloud, and the lights of the Folly's cottages were glowing.

As we gathered near the shop we heard Teresa singing, and the rosy smell of fresh bath-salts drifted over to us and hung in the night air. She came out presently wearing a newly ironed summer frock, but no one made a move to join her until she spotted us and called us over. Close to this rinsed and lovely woman, our jealousies bloomed in the dark, and she gave us quick curious glances as if our smouldering desires had in some way communicated themselves to her.

The ramshackle tourer that carried some of the surf club men and their girls stopped at the GO SLOW sign, and Teresa flashed another puzzled look at us. Perhaps we had betrayed our tension by all drawing in our breaths at one moment. The tourer started down the zigzag, but halted briefly where we had placed each sign, and with each stop came shouts and laughter.

"What, for goodness' sake, is happening up there?" said Teresa, fortunately looking to the hillside and not into our guilty eyes.

We had not planned for this.

Teresa kept peering up to the hillside. "There seems to be something stuck there," she said. "And whatever are they laughing at?"

They were soon outside the shop telling Teresa, five men and three girls in this ancient hoodless tourer, all of them full of weekend high spirits that had been bolstered by a stop at the Dog's Hind Leg.

"Who's trying to put the brakes on Fearless?" asked one of the men.

"The brakes on Fearless?" questioned Teresa.

"Go Slow . . . Dangerous Bend . . . Loose Gravel . . . Pot Holes . . ." said the man with a backward wave to the zigzag road and our signs. "The whole road's strung with them from top to bottom, and some of the spelling is choice!"

Even this did not immediately point the finger at us. Teresa swung around and eyed in turn the lights from the shacks of Shellback O'Leary and Fingers Galore. "Which of those two did it, I wonder. Or . . . " She petered out as she swung the other way so that her accusation was aimed at Lady Hodge's mansion. "It could be her ladyship's housekeeper. She's often complained to me that their wisp of a dog gets hysterics at the sound of the motor-bike."

We had never seen Teresa in this fiercely protective role before. We were starting to believe that we had made a ghastly mistake when one of the men pointed at us and said: "Hey, you lot wouldn't be responsible for this, would you?"

As Teresa whirled to face us, we stood as five variations on the theme of mute guilt. Bandy McAnsh had indeed been prophetic when he dubbed us distress signals.

"Did you really do it?" she asked.

We owned up to this with nods, hard swallows and sickly grins, as the car-load of weekenders shrieked laughter into our faces.

"I'll be blowed!" she said, resorting to one of Fearless' comments. "Why?"

We looked desperately at one another for a spokesman.

"Will someone please explain? Come along, Spark."

"Aw, we just thought we'd sorta slow him down,"

said Spark with a shrug, while we all collected another broadside of laughter from the tourer.

" 'E could skid over the edge," explained Fido, "an' drown hisself."

"Oh, so you were protecting him?"

"Sort of," said Fido. "Yeah: Protectin' 'im!"

One of the men found that laughter alone could not express his amusement, so he banged on the side of the car with the edge of his fist.

And then Teresa began to join the laughter. "He's in for a shock, isn't he?"

The tourer headed across to the rear of the pavilion, where the weekenders unloaded bedding and food. We relaxed in Teresa's company as we waited. Her approval somehow seemed to ensure that the operation would be successful.

About the expected time, Fearless was poised on the throbbing motor-bike high above us. The headlamp's beam was levelled at the first of the road signs, and it looked like the silhouette of a sunflower caught in the dark.

"He's seen it," said Teresa, her husky tone a measure of the intense excitement we all shared.

The roar of the engine dwindled away as Fearless took in the warning, and at that moment we were entitled to believe that our plan was going to work. But only for that moment.

In bursts fast rising in fury, the motor-bike's roar reached such a pitch that it might have been a tornado giving notice that it was about to unleash itself on the valley and lay it in ruins. The fevered quivering of the poised beam seemed to indicate that it was being saturated with extra candle-power and that it was all set to erupt into a raging flood of light and so act as the signal to the high wind to start rampaging.

This was the sixth time we had witnessed Fearless' arrival — four on Friday nights and one on New Year's Eve — but never one charged with as much abandon as this.

Each of our road signs was treated with scorn by a white-hot lick of headlamp as the beam lit up its puny demand. Each seemed to provoke Fearless to hurtle at greater speed. Teresa gave tiny gasps of horror at his increasing recklessness. We all looked sick. To shock us more, from the back of the surf club pavilion came ecstatic cheers.

On the second last turn there was a loud shower of rubble down the hillside into the water. Then the last turn, and Fearless zoomed across on to the flat. We flew into the garden in front of the shop as he braked with a taunting shout, sand leaping as the rear wheel of the machine kicked around.

The engine stopped, but Fearless laughed on. It was the sort of pitch he reached when he tried to tell a joke. This time we had provided the joke, leaving him free to laugh. He might have gone on longer, but for Fingers Galore. The piano-player implied that, while he had enjoyed the performance, he considered it time to finish. From the cave came "God Save the King". It might just as easily have been "God Save Fearless".

20 Fearless had another attack of laughing the next morning. He came outside the shop and pointed to a scribble of cloud somewhere over Serenity. Was somebody else telling a joke on his behalf? And writing it in the sky?

He squeezed an explanation between laughs: "There goes Cyclone!"

"Cyclone Jones?" we asked, remembering how he had mentioned one of his partners on the Wall of Death.

"That's him."

We peered. Then we spotted a midge flying ahead of the scribble, and Fearless calmed himself enough to tell us that Cyclone Jones had graduated from being a rider on a Wall of Death to a weekend signwriter. We were too far away to be able to read what he was spelling out to the Saturday crowds gathered on the beach at Serenity, but as we squinted and strained our eyes we might have been peering into the future and trying to see which of five names was being announced to the world.

"Up we go, down we go, around we go!" cried Spark, using the trailer for the Wall of Death in honour of the antics of Cyclone Jones.

Teresa called to Fearless to help her carry the big umbrella down on to the beach, and we withdrew to the battlements in the sandhills. The writing in the sky expanded into long wraiths, and I viewed it through the picture-frame, but no words could be identified. Then I used this private window to watch Teresa and Fearless. They spread themselves on the sand under the wide pale-green umbrella. It cast shade tinged with the kind of underwater luminosity that we found in the lake of lupins. Room enough surely between them for five and a half stone of small boy.

Unfortunately, it was clear to me that other units, ranging from Fido's four stone nothing to Spark's six and a bit, were toying with the same thought. It was not surprising, therefore, that more and more imaginary scenes should replace reality within the sides of that picture-frame. The tawny sand of the beach became the walls and pillars of the church in Serenity. A touch of stained glass threw sad plum and purple tints. Heart-rending organ music, played by Fingers Galore, out of a long retirement for this tragic occasion. Tall beeswax candles alight in bodyguard-size brass candlesticks, four small coffins draped with flags from the McAnsh sleeping-hut. Here were the mortal remains of four departed distress signals: Maps Prior, Misty Hayward, Spark Monahan, Fido Ward. Poor lads, they had been betrayed by a tin canoe, tipped over, sucked down, then cast up drowned at the feet of Socrates the horse. I appointed myself chief mourner, battling to hold back a flood of hot tears, Teresa on one side fondling my hand, Fearless on the other with his hand like a giant epaulette on my shoulder.

At least the deaths of these four companions had been brought about by an accident. As yet I had not started to imagine murder.

21 The game became grimmer now, each of us somehow taking turns to contribute an item to a weird and protracted sort of concert.

Misty was located after another disappearance with blood running from scratches on his hands and forearms. We knew at once what had happened. He had been trying to sneak a lead on us in the play for the role of Teresa's choice. She had mentioned she would like to make a pet of one of the wild cat's kittens. The mother cat had obviously objected.

We encouraged Teresa to talk, and as we sat around on the sand after our daily swimming lesson, she filled in the backgrounds of Fearless and herself. She told us more about the Wall of Death.

"Those were mad days," she said, and her use of one of Spark's favourite words had the rest of us instantly wary of him. "But I honestly think Fearless was glad to give up the riding. He was always too big, for one thing. And he was past his best. Sometimes I think he comes down that hillside as he does just to prove that he hasn't entirely lost his touch." She paused to picture his Friday night dash, and then went on. "He's an unusual man under all his fun and easy ways, a very unusual man indeed. There's no malice in him. He's a man quite without malice."

Was it true that she had suffered an accident on the Wall of Death?

"Oh yes. It began with a bit of cigarette ash, and I did the rest."

Cigarette ash?

"Someone was smoking up top. It got in my eye."

"Was you 'urt bad?"

"It took me three months in hospital to get over it. Poor Fearless . . ."

She conveyed to us in various ways that her whole life centred around her husband. For instance, the way she so fondly used some of his expressions. But then she sometimes borrowed Sparks' way of saying things! Did this show where her preference would lie? Twitches of hope and despair were touched off when she dropped her h's as Fido did, or confronted us with a sharp Maps-style question.

Once, as we lay at her feet like the markings on the sundial, the opening chords of a throttled masterpiece came from the cave on the southern side of the bay. Teresa sighed. "I don't always see eye to eye with Shellback O'Leary, but I really do wish we could hear something not quite so classical. Perhaps he's never heard of 'Tiptoe through the Tulips' or 'I'm Painting the Clouds with Sunshine'."

It was my privilege to find out about this.

*

No one needed to explain how the nickname of Fingers Galore had originated. Every day he stood outside his shack and held up one or both hands at about ear level and slowly wriggled the fingers. He might have been conversing to someone in the distance in sign language, like the deaf-and-dumb lay nuns at St Roderick's, but it was part exercise, part nervous habit. By a sort of optical illusion he seemed to treble the number of fingers on each hand.

To get within talking distance of this recluse involved a number of ticklish moves. I had to detach myself from seven sharp eyes, and I had to reach the grey-and-glass fronted shack without being spotted. Otherwise there would be five of us. Necessity is the mother of much cunning.

A roundabout approach seemed best. I inched up the zigzag road, keeping close to the clay and rock wall, till I reached the elbow directly above the shack. Fido and Misty were lying in the sandhills and keeping a watch on the shop. Spark and Maps were moving across from Shellback's end of the beach, and pretty soon there would be a conference concerning my whereabouts. I used a dip in the hillside to cloak my descent. The hot sun screamed down at me. The waves cocked wild, white, tell-tale fingers towards me. However, I reached the ledge below, unseen from the sandhills, even though the conference was growing worried and four heads were doing quick turns the full swing of the compass.

"Choker! Where are ya? Cho-kerr!"

They headed up past the island of pines, no doubt hoping to locate me in the abandoned camp, where I had set up a studio for finger-painting on old board with tar and whitewash. Once they were far enough away to say good day to the sunflowers, I stepped out from behind a shaggy shoulder of rock and found myself a few yards away from the glass double doors and the grey facade of the inlet's musical cave. It looked very cosy in there: carpets, easy-chairs, a piano like a big harp boxed in and propped up parallel to the ground. Shellback was wrong. There were no barnacles on the keys.

A scuffing sound brought me right around: the gentleman himself out on the ledge. He had been there all the time, but I had been too concerned with my four companions to notice him.

He had a stringy, smoked-fish look about him, and his pipe seemed to be keeping him in this condition with puffs of grey and pale blue. Some of the penetrating sting was taken out of his eyes by the smoke as it drifted in front of his face, but I was uncomfortable in his presence. At first I found it impossible to speak, but when I sprang the lock in my throat the words tumbled out: "Mister, could you play 'Tiptoe through the Tulips'?"

He took the pipe from his mouth, and the smoke rose to one side of him. He was a foreigner, all right. "Yunk man," he said in a stifled way that suggested an enlarged Adam's apple might be troubling him, "I-ee do nut tiptoe."

"How about playing 'I'm Painting the Clouds with Sunshine'?"

"I-ee do nut — paint."

That was that. I retreated in a panicky run along the track to the beach, and in my wake came a loud defiance from the piano, as if Fingers Galore was using strong music to banish the impurities left hanging around his abode by my vulgar requests.

The ambergris started all five of us on the same search.

At one of the drying-off sessions after the swimming

lessons, Teresa told us how ambergris was disgorged by whales, and that it was highly valued because of its importance in the making of expensive perfumes. A small lump of it would solve the money problems of setting up the house Fearless planned nearer the source of his work. Find the ambergris, and a place under the rooftop of that house could be assured.

And so we were all out early to greet the seagulls, laying footprints in the sand that had been smoothed out by the tide overnight. Rushed investigations revealed wads of cotton waste or decaying fish heads or shipwrecked jellyfish or barnacle-encrusted hunks of cork, anything but ambergris; which was not surprising as it is disgorged only by sperm whales, and I have discovered since that no whale of this species frequents that coastline.

Teresa's whims were thus our commands.

"That poor man," she said one day, looking across to Double Martin's cottage, where the shells lay unchanged in his front garden. "I've often wished those words could be changed. Yet what could we put in its place?"

Her eyes had a translucent green that I had seen in the sea water near the rocks, and she looked at us one by one for an answer. This was a difficult challenge. Meanwhile, in other ways we kept trying to impress her and so win that escape from the regime of St Roderick's.

22 Spark's master bid was somehow related in terms of abandon to Fearless' Friday night arrivals, and it began near the top of the sledge run we had established on the northern side of the bay, close above Shellback's cave.

He had salvaged the remains of a giant box-kite from

the rubbish-dump, and as he nailed it onto the sledge we gathered around.

Maps opening the firing: "Who are ya gonna crucify?"

Spark gaped up at him.

It was not usual for Maps to score so well. He himself seemed surprised, and there was a twitch at the side of his mouth that might have developed into a smirk in someone with a less masked face.

"How mad can you get?" said Spark, but for him it was a tame retort.

"That's a cross you're makin', ain't it?" went on Maps, and Fido showed that he regarded himself as the most likely victim by getting set to bolt.

Could it be that Spark was proposing to reduce the field and the competition? There was some sort of crossbeam being nailed onto the sledge.

"I'm not making no cross," averred Spark, but still quietly.

"Looks like a cross t'me. An' what are them big nails for? Look at 'em!"

They were monsters. Fido gave another jerk. Misty turned his head side-on, as if hoping to hide himself behind the pane of opaque glass.

"They're for the wings," said Spark, and his chirp came back. "The ding-diddle-lings!"

"Y'mean the hands?" said Maps.

A bigger jerk from Fido. Misty shrank further behind the spectacle pane. I felt a little cold. By the setting of the sun we could be one less in number.

"No," said Spark, enjoying Maps's insinuations now. "They're for the wings, like I just said. I'm taking off!"

"Taking off what?"

"This is gonna be a glider. Ida the spider!"

"Y-don't mean —"

Maps was the startled party now as Spark used a hammer like a blackboard pointer to show how he would sweep down the slope of the sledge run to the edge of a low precipice — and then farther.

"Whee!" he cried. "I'm goin' sailing right out there. Skim over th' waves! Land on the beach!"

"You sure are mad," breathed Maps.

"You bet. I'm barmy. Barm!-diddle-arm!-darm-darm!-army!"

This made kidnapping wild kittens or searching for ambergris or requesting distinguished pianists for popular tunes of the day seem puny stratagems. Compared with Spark, we were half-moons alongside a blazing sun.

"Hurrum! Hoo! Hee! Haw!" Spark chanted on, now using his auctioneering warm-up to time out the hitting in of another nail.

"Y'll break ya neck!"

"Haw-hah! Haw-hah! Going! Going! Gone!" And the nail was struck home.

"I said — y'll break ya neck!"

"Break a record. Tha'ts-a what-a I'll-a break-a! Whee-diddle-dee!" Again Spark used the hammer to describe the path of his flight. If he pulled off this stunt he would fly out of our clutches into the arms of Teresa.

Maps did not approve of the way Fido, Misty and I had been awed to silence. He addressed us contemptuously: "Let him do it. That'll mean one less of us."

Only Maps could voice our secret thoughts without a flicker of feeling. Still, it released a certain black excitement in me.

"Ya better make ya will," Maps suggested. "Y'll have a cracked neck after ya hit the water."

"Here," said Spark, handing over his pocket-knife with the produce merchant's name on it. "Hang on to it. If the glider don't work, you can have it, and with my very best compliments."

That knife was his sole possession. We considered our clothes the property of St Roderick's. We had nothing that we could call our own. Schoolbooks were hand-me-downs, like the basic facts of life. The things with which we played were trolleys and worn car tyres, and the use of them was based on a crude but effective system. As we broke free of the classrooms there would be shouts of "Bags I the motor tyre!" or "I bags the trolley!" Whoever got in first was deemed owner for the current play period. It has a parallel in a game called Grab, and it is not so very different from the way nations have claimed continents in the past.

Spark hammered on, securing the main wings and then a tail section, with nails scavenged from under the hull of Tubby Porter's boat. He was without fear; either that or incapable of suffering from it.

His abandon did not abate as he positioned the contraption at the brink of the sledge run. He was about to step on board a flying funeral pyre. He faced us with a fiendish grin and blazing blue eyes.

"I'm morf!"

"Are you gonna kiss anyone goodbye?" inquired Maps, coldly still.

"I'll shake hands," Spark said, shooting out a grubby paw, its nails thickly ringed with black, so that he seemed already marked for death.

Maps gave him a limp shake in return. Fido clutched his hands behind his back and edged farther away, as if fearing that this madness might be contagious. Misty shook, but dazedly, and his good pane clouded up with perspiration. I felt that I might be touching death, and the black excitement froze my jaws. Spark should have been carrying the diagonally-divided red and yellow flag that we had identified in the code book as meaning *Man Overboard*. He was partly prepared for the water as, like the rest of us, he was wearing his bathing-costume, but I did not feel that the rooster on the *Excelsior Flour* emblem was likely to have anything victorious to crow about.

At this point, Spark himself started to crow, cupping his hands around his mouth as he let out cries such as the marshalling hands made in the saleyards besides St Roderick's.

"Garn! Getcha! Gorn! Gore!"

The cries were multiplied scores of times by the folds and clefts of the bay and the valley. Teresa came out to the front of the shop and shaded her eyes as she looked in our direction. Fingers Galore emerged out of the afternoon shadows on to his rocky ledge. Now that Spark had secured Teresa's attention, he lay on the sledge and pushed it over the brink with his feet. It started down the grassy incline on its polished runners, the wings flumping clumsily either side, and his "Whee-ee!" rang on our ears like a death clarion.

Part of the thrill of sledging had been the way we had to slew around before reaching the edge that hung over the water at a point nearer the headland than Shellback's ledge. There was a patch of unflattened grass right at the edge, but Spark's contraption swept through this and hung free of anything solid for a moment before toppling over and out of sight, to the accompaniment of a frightened cry from Teresa, followed shortly by a bellow from Shellback.

As Teresa raced through the gap in the sandhills and across the sand on her way to the rocks, we went fearfully to the grassy edge. We expected to find Spark laid out on a rock, crushed like a fish for the wild cats by Socrates the horse. We were all partly to blame: we had wished Spark's end.

First we saw the wings and the sledge, the swells nudging them shoreward. As for the valiant Spark, he was doing a dog-paddle in the water, like one of the nuns at St Roderick's rolling wool from a skein. Shellback was offering him the tip of a long bamboo rod. Spark grasped it, and in this way he was hauled ashore. He showed no outward sign of injury.

We had to make a detour to get down from the grassy slope, and by this time Teresa had arrived and was the kneeling half of a combination that made the four of us feel sick with defeat. Even though he had taken a strange and dangerous route, Spark had flown into her arms all right. He was drenched, but Teresa was oblivious to the way the water made dark splotches on her pink summer frock. She held him by the shoulders and she shook him gently, trying to get an answer from him.

"Does it hurt anywhere? Are you all right? Please, Spark, tell me!"

Spark did not seem conscious of what he had done or where he was. His lids were heavy as if from sleep. He did not seem to recognise us. Shellback glared at him with fierce regularity in between rocking around on the edges of his horny feet to cast sharp solicitous looks out to where he believed the lair of Henry the groper to be.

"Spark, darling!" Another gentle shake. The tussle among us was as good as over now. She had called him "darling". When the time came to pack up our bathing-costumes and pyjamas and don our Sunday boots for the return to St Roderick's we would be leaving Spark Monahan behind.

Teresa was close to tears as she spoke to Shellback. "He can't talk."

"In that case he'll grow up to be the first dumb auctioneer the world has ever known."

"Haven't you any feelings?"

"I wuz nearly devoid av thim for all time, Missus." He pointed shoreward to where the wings and the sledge rocked farther apart on the crest of another passing swell. "A hit on the head be thit lump av whativer it might be, an' I'd be gettin' introduced to the hereafter. Lad," he went on, addressing Spark, "if ye're intent upon turnin' yeself into a lump av bait, will ye come to me first so's I kin attach a strong fishin'-line to ye tail? In that way I'll enjoy the benefit av ye hare-brain should ye be nabbed be Henry."

"Shellback, hush!" Teresa demanded.

"I've spoken me mind," he said, folding his arms and concentrating his gaze seaward.

"Are you awlaright?" pleaded Teresa, using one of Spark's favourite drawls.

Now he became aware of where he was and what he had achieved. The suggestion of sleep about his eyes was replaced by a sort of smugly impish wonder. He flickered a glance of recognition towards us as he set about formally accepting his triumph. "You bet," he said.

"Are you quite sure?"

"Course!" It was as if he had brought the hammer down on the biggest auction of a lifetime.

Teresa gave him a long look. She took her hands from his shoulders. Spark was puzzled. So were we. The softness was going out of her eyes. "You're lucky," she said, "very, very lucky. Don't you ever dare try doing anything like that again."

"Here y'are!" said Maps, smartly handing back the

pocket-knife; but what he really meant was "An interesting try, but you're one of us again."

23 On their sober nights the McAnshes had us headed for the sleeping-hut soon after we finished our household duties. We began to feel something of the locked-away atmosphere of St Roderick's, until we realised that the solution lay up the valley not far from a sundial that gave by day the time of night in places such as Rome and Timbuktoo.

It was a pity that we could not pay Sundial Watson the compliment of telling him how beautifully effective his wine could be, what quaint nostalgics it could stir out of Mrs McAnsh, how Bandy could take one of his wife's remarks and twist it around into something that sounded the same but meant almost nothing.

One bottle led to another. At the back of the McAnsh cottage rose a small stack of stoppered empties, while in Sundial Watson's shed the shelves became noticeably lightened. We reached the point when we realised that no more bottles could be filched without insulting Sundial's powers of observation.

The McAnshes brewed their tea in a big enamel pot, on which black showed where the white had been chipped off. Part of our rostered duties included the emptying of this noble utensil. It was Maps who suggested, as he tipped out the swill, that if we watered it down to the right tint and drained out all the leaves we would have a liquid of the same pale hue as the pumpkin wine. And so the empties behind the cottage were dusted and polished, the cold tea carefully strained and watered, then funnelled into the bottles, stoppered and sneaked back on to the shelves in Sundial's shed, behind the bottles of real wine.

Misty's eye was no longer the only blind one among us. We assumed that our filching would stay undiscovered until such time as we were on the way back to St Roderick's, but that was a miscalculation, as we realised when Sundial came down the hill at a grotesque, rolling half-run, as if it was so long since he had tried to run that to do it properly he would have to learn how all over again. He carried a full bottle from his shed, and his immediate destination was the McAnsh cottage. This was our cue to uproot ourselves from among the tussocks in the sandhills and move to a point that would enable us to eavesdrop and at the same time make a quick escape. Our ears were open to their maximum, like the ice-plant flowers under the hot noon blaze.

Sundial seemed to proclaim rather than speak, so we had no difficulty in hearing him when he opened up to the McAnshes: "I am going to ask a very special favour of you both. I wonder, would you taste a little of this wine?"

"That's not such an unusual thing to ask," said Mrs McAnsh, as guilt chilled us. "Is it, my dear?"

"Never at all," murmured Bandy.

We checked the escape route: behind the bushes and up the hillside. We heard the squeal of a cupboard opening, the clink of glasses, the burble of liquid being poured.

"May I say," said Sundial over the pouring, "that never in all my years of making wine have I produced anything quite so unexpected as this."

"Health!" Bandy was heard to say.

"Yes, indeed," said his wife.

Our ears bloomed even bigger as we waited for it, and

right on time, which was almost immediately, came the double splutter, the double cough.

"Forgive us, please," Mrs McAnsh gushed. "Perhaps it's a little early in the day for us to be partaking."

"Ah, but don't I understand the reason for your — er — surprise," suggested Sundial with a sort of desperate eagerness.

"Why should we be surprised?" answered Mrs McAnsh with crafty coyness. "Dear me, we know your wine so very, very well. Isn't that so, my dear?"

"Ever so," said Bandy.

"Surely, surely," pleaded Sundial, "surely you detect something a little different?"

"Not at all, Mr Watson. And I'm certain my husband agrees." She spoke louder and pointedly and may well have accompanied her reassurance with a kick under the table at one of Bandy's hoop shins. "It's up to Mr Watson's standard, don't you think so?"

"Quality," pronounced Bandy.

Sundial sounded frantic. "You don't detect anything different then?"

"Mr Watson, I've been in the liquor trade myself — on the administrative side as you might say — and I assure you that this wine is well up to the standard set by your pumpkin."

"No change at all?" inquired Sundial limply.

"None. What do you say, my dear?"

"No, no, never a bit," Bandy assured him. "Upon my wretched soul, no."

"Then whatever has happened to my sense of taste?"

"The palate can be a very strange thing. Most contrary, Mr Watson."

"Extraordinary. I could swear this tasted like . . ."

"Now what did it taste like to you?" inquired Mrs McAnsh in a cloying motherly way as Sundial hesitated, and I remembered Shellback saying on our first day at Captain's Folly that the McAnshes were just the pair to give us a lesson in how to live on our wits.

"No, no, in view of the kind opinions you have given me, it would be most discourteous of me to say it. Most. However, I trust you will not count me unduly rude if I take this bottle elsewhere to seek another seasoned opinion."

This seemed to worry Mrs McAnsh. "Oh, but why should you be at all upset if your palate seems to have played you wrong with this one bottle?"

"My dear Mrs McAnsh, I have already tried out *two* other bottles, and the contents therein taste exactly the same!"

The McAnshes had no counter to this, and Sundial emerged from the cottage with the bottle of bogus pumpkin, his beard jogging as if reinforced with a wad of the steel wool we used on the pots and pans.

His search for another seasoned opinion took him straight to Shellback's ledge, and we were close on hand as Sundial received the answer to his opening request.

"Yis, yis, I'd be tellin' a lie if I said I wuz not partial to a drink. And I've no intention av insultin' ye, Watson, but mebbe it'd be best for the relations between the two av us if I didn't partake. Best for ye feelings, I mean. I niver like t'have to insult a fella straight to his face."

"My good Mr O'Leary, I merely want your expert judgment. Please now. Only a sip. That should be ample."

"Be the saints, 'twill be more thin ample!"

"You'll oblige, then?"

"Give me the bottle." He agreed, but with weary reluctance.

Sundial handed over the unstoppered bottle and

Shellback wiped the mouth with the heel of his hand and inspected the contents before putting them to the test. He took a large swig. Suddenly his eyes protruded through the button-holes of skin in a way that we had never seen before, and his cheeks and the top of his head turned into a ripe reddish-brown. He swallowed, and then came the slightly delayed explosion: "Sweet Satan!"

"What is it, Mr O'Leary? What do you detect?"

A thunderous "What do I detect?"

"Yes, Mr O'Leary?" Nervous expectancy.

"I detect cold bloody tea!"

"That's what I say!" cried Sundial, raising his pith helmet triumphantly.

"Ye do?" hollered Shellback with mountainous incredulity.

"I do, indeed." He retrieved the bottle with a near snatch. "Tea. Cold tea! Don't you perceive what that means, Mr O'Leary?"

"Yis, av course I do," replied Shellback with a prompt nod. "Whan ye were fillin' up the bottles, ye were pourin' the wine down ye sink. Be mistake ye emptied cold tea inta the bottle."

"No, no, no, not at all. This is a discovery parallel to that which the ancient alchemists sought for so long. How to convert lead into gold."

Shellback's scrutiny of the other became a sort of instant insanity test. "Watson, I said it wuz not me wish to insult ye, an' that I meant. With all due respect to ye great discovery, what ye've done is equivalent to turnin' gold inta somethin' akin to lead."

"We shall see, we shall see. I intend to take immediate steps to register my discovery. I shall take out the necessary patent rights. Indeed, I may yet travel to the other side of the world again before I die. And I shan't forget you, Mr O'Leary, I shan't. After all, you were the first to confirm the truth of my good fortune.''

Shellback acknowledged this with a pinch-mouthed nod as Sundial moved off, the precious bottle tucked under his arm. As he passed us he raised his pith helmet. It extracted a short astonished laugh from Maps, which in itself was something of an accomplishment.

Shellback welcomed an audience. ''I've bin a good manny years in this place, an' if I had to count all the idiots I've encountered on the fingers av me two hands, thin I'd soon be runnin' out av fists. Frind Watson is what ye might call an idiot's idiot. In the days av the Depression there were boys here capable av concoctin' brews that could blow up railway lines. It wuz only recommended that ye should consume them in the case av extreme emergency, but they were av some use. What use is cold tea?''

''You could always boil it up and drink it hot,'' Spark suggested.

''A right lot av muck that would be, too,'' glowered Shellback. ''Av course, the poor fella's t'be pitied. Manny years ago he wint for a world cruise on a ship. I'm told he coincided his visit to Naples with an eruption av the local volcano and got himself hit on the head with a piece av flyin' rock. Mebbe in truth it wuz a flower-pot off a window-sill, but iver since he's bin livin' his life upside-down as it were.'' He said this with his eyes following Sundial's return up the valley. He faced us now. ''Tell me this, if ye can. How the divil did all thit cold tea get inta that bottle?''

No one cared to enlighten Shellback, and as we left him Misty had something to say to us. ''There musta been a time in this place when it rained flower-pots on just about everyone.''

In due course Sundial was informed that there were

no commercial prospects in his discovery. It would be cheaper to make tea in the usual way than produce pumpkin wine and await some mysterious transmutation. And so whenever we passed close enough to glimpse the bronze finger on his sundial we saw a somewhat puzzled face hovering nearby beneath the pith helmet.

Those road signs we had set up were never systematically removed. As the weeks passed they were knocked down, blown over, tilted and twisted, and every time I saw them I was reminded of another dangerous escapade — the stealing of the wine. Especially when we began to repeat the first filching.

24 Some time before this there were other crises. For instance, Fido had begun his major bid to install himself as Teresa's favourite.

Of the five of us he seemed to have the surest grounds for guessing what his father might have been. A fisherman, surely. Fido had a gift for catching fish in the way that Spark was a natural talker and I had a talent for drawing.

The craze for fishing began after we found the cache of bamboo rods and tackle in one of the huts of the abandoned camp. It became a daily affair on the rocks and ledges opposite Shellback's shack. Here we headed as soon as our duties around the McAnsh household were finished, and for a week or so we were often still there when the ocean was flooded with sunset. We fell asleep with water winking before our eyes, and with our first breaths on waking in the morning came the longing to be back on the hunt again.

We caught small herrings, brown tiddlers so slimy that they were difficult to hold, and a yellow and white fish with brown spots that was called a guffey. At the end of each day's sport, when the catches were laid out and counted, Fido was always the winner. By some nameless magic the fish were doomed to fall in greater numbers to his hooks, even though ours might have been more carefully baited, more deliberately cast. At first he seemed worried that he should possess powers beyond the rest of us, but by the end of the day he was yelling out his score and declaring himself the victor, and, since this was the sort of thing that might win him Teresa's exclusive approval, we withdrew from fishing altogether and left him without any competition.

No doubt this was something of a relief to Shellback O'Leary. He had been keeping a long watch on us from his ledge, or through a window. We had no designs on Henry the groper, not simply because this fish seemed his exclusive property. Henry was in the class of big-game fishing and we were not equipped for that. Besides, we had seen the tawny-green-grey drifting shape that Shellback said was Henry, and we assumed that he did not appear on the side of the bay from which we tried our luck.

And so it seemed that the craze for fishing was over.

But not for Fido.

Late one afternoon, when the tide was full and the sea mild, he launched the tin canoe from the rocks on the southern side of the bay. He was alone in it as he used the paddle, a square of wood nailed to a length of broom handle, to push away from the rocks. He dipped the paddle into the water on either side in the gaps between the tin and the outriggers, and propelled the canoe to a point that brought it roughly over what was believed to be the site of the wrecked sailing ship. I remembered that he had spent some days trying to be alone on a grassy ledge high above the bay, and now — with Spark, Maps and Misty — I saw the result of his research.

Watch out, Shellback!

The wrecked sailing ship was assumed to be the lair of Henry the groper, and in the sandhills four of us were certain what Fido was doing out there, and naturally each of us wished him the very best of bad luck as he baited a small line and dropped it over the side. It disgusted us to see how soon he whipped a wriggling fillet of silver out of the sea, and presently this went over the side on a big hook attached to a thick line — tackle that Fido had also found in the abandoned camp.

The canoe was lifted gently on swells that went on to become polite waves; and as these swells passed, the outriggers patted the water either side into brief ripplings. We looked across to Shellback's shack. The door was half-open, but there was no sign of the inmate.

Fido gave a quick upward tug of the line, and Spark decided that Shellback should be warned.

"Mis-ter O'Lear-ree!"

The echo had the effect of bouncing Shellback into the doorway, his pipe in his mouth. We had noted — perhaps because of Mrs McAnsh's way of dividing drinkers into categories — that on either side of the bay there were contrasting approaches to pipe-smoking. Fingers Galore could build a wraith of smoke and stand in the middle of it. Shellback usually puffed hard, and now the smoke came fast, as if from a locomotive going uphill.

Another tug on the line from Fido jerked the pipe out of Shellback's mouth.

"Hey!" he bawled. "You out there!"

Fido now showed that he had taken some lessons from Misty in how to ignore an irate audience. He calmly fished on.

"You out there! You in thit tin tub!"

Fido gave a bigger tug, and Shellback raised both fists, one holding on to the smouldering pipe, like a native rainmaker about to go into a tribal dance.

"Don't try iny av thit deaf-eared business on me, damn ye! Git ashore before ye're sunk an' drowned! Have ye no regard for ye own life?" He paused, while Fido crouched unruffled in the canoe. "Answer me, dammit!"

Teresa was in the sandhills behind us, drawn from the shop by Shellback's shouting, while Fingers Galore was out on his ledge.

"Git t'blazes out av there!" bawled Shellback, giving up any pretence of concern for Fido's life. " 'Tis poachin'! Trespassin'!"

Suddenly the line was taut and Fido was upright in the boat, making one of the outriggers dip deeply in the water as he pulled his hardest. Something was holding the hook down below. Then it was slack again and Fido had to sit down abruptly to prevent himself falling overboard. He hauled in the line. The hook was bare.

"He's got a nerve, hasn't he?" said Teresa, joining us and making it all the more nauseating to watch Fido baiting a small hook and dropping it over the side. Almost immediately he began to play small bites. It was unfair that he should be gifted in this way.

Shellback twitched with every nibble, and whenever I think back to this incident I feel that all five of us shared the guilt for the torment that man endured. The sun was low and it caught the furze on his shoulders and back in such a way that he appeared to be carrying some symbolical grey burden of old age.

Fido soon had another herring for the big hook, and while he prepared the heavy line Shellback warned Henry of the danger. He grabbed up the piece of iron and belted the metal hoop of the motor-car tyre-rim, believing that muffled clangs would reach down to the groper. Fido remained unperturbed and the big hook, freshly baited, went over the side again.

Shellback stood grinding the outer edges of his feet into the rock surface. When Fido pulled the line taut again, he became frantic. This time he did not bang the hoop. Instead he yelled across the bay. "You over there!" he hollered, cupping his hands around his mouth, then waving furiously to attract further attention to himself from Fingers Galore. " 'Tis a theory av mine thit ye've bin able t'warn the groper with ye piano-playin'! Will ye thump out a few wild notes for me now? A few wild notes!"

Fingers Galore looked behind him quickly just to make sure it was him Shellback was addressing and not someone of miraculously quaint accomplishment near-by. Even at a distance we were aware of the gaping incredulity on the lanky man's face.

"Quick now! Thit young divil out there happens t'be an expert at catchin' fish!"

Beside us, Teresa breathed: "Too late. Fido's got something."

Whatever had latched onto the hook was threatening to drag Fido and the canoe under the water. Fido was still the smallest of us, but there was no fence wire in his arms now. He tugged fiercely and the canoe tipped to the edges of its freeboard.

"For Gawd's sake, man!" Shellback bawled in outraged despair. "Rachmaninoff! Paderewski! Iny mortal thing ye kin thump out!"

But Fingers Galore was ignoring Shellback and following Fido's tussle. He had something on the line, and it needed all his strength to haul it on board.

"That ain't Henry!" shouted Maps, a cry of fiendish triumph.

No, it looked more like a giant eel — long, brown and slimy — until it was recognised as nothing more deadly than a hank of seaweed.

"What a shame," sighed Teresa, expressing much too much sympathy for our comfort; but at least she had no cause as yet to celebrate with cartwheels in Fido's honour.

It took some moments of hard staring for Shellback to identify what the sea had given up in place of Henry. He warmed himself up with some mirthless cackles before indulging in an outburst of derisive relief. "Why don't ye dress yeself up in thit seaweed muck! Make yeself a hat and put ye schemin' young head inta it! Leave that groper to thim thit are entitled to fish him out av the sea!" He put a fresh light to his pipe and the puffs of smoke he blew were big grey raspberries.

Fido dumped the seaweed. Before he paddled back to the rocks he wiped his fingers on the front of his bathing-costume. But he might have been simply freshening up the crowing rooster of the *Excelsior Flour* brand.

25 The best part of another week passed, including a weekend market by Fearless trying to get a joke fully told before he was completely swamped by his own laughter. It became the occasion for a sinister laughing competition among the five so-called December boys as each tried to prove himself the most appreciative.

This brought Fearless' laughter (and story) to a stop. He stared at us as if we were out of our minds. "Blow me down! I didn't think it was as funny as all that."

We had exposed the blackness in our hearts. That false and forced laughter was part of the mark of Cain we all secretly carried because of our murderous thoughts. We had each committed mass fratricide, but so far in our minds only. Now we were to discover that one of us might well be capable of doing away with the others should the chance arise.

This discovery was made one day when we found ourselves on the northern headland of the bay.

Up and down the coastline grim promontories overlapped one another: sloping gorilla foreheads, flattened boxers' noses, shovel chins awash in the froth of the Pacific. We reached the headland after passing caves still partly boarded across the front from the days of the Depression. We looked down into tiny coves where the sea rattled the pebbles and made noises like the marbles in the drum used to decide the raffles at the church bazaars.

Neither of the two headlands was to be trusted. Long ago they had conspired to trick the skipper of a sailing ship into wrecking his command. A few trees clung here, all of them stunted, their limbs twisted as if frozen at the height of some seizure. The rock itself looked evil, scorched red and purple rock contorted into hollows and caves. According to Shellback this was the result of molten volcanic rock meeting the sea. Start a few bonfires here and get the area well hazed over with smoke and it would be the sort of terrain I expected to find in Purgatory. Naturally I hoped to dodge the fires of Hell, but I had resigned myself to a stretch in the purifying regions of that halfway halt for seasoned sinners.

Among the hollows and caves were holes that led to black caverns, some of them down under our feet, perhaps fashioned by a prehistoric glass-blower who was forced to work in murky lava. We knelt and cocked our ears over holes pouted like scabbed lips and heard the sound of the sea as a growl or a moan or an uneasy hum.

On the northern headland was a small hole that led to a black whispering gallery. We had discerned something pale in its depths, but we did not identify what this was until that day our murderous potentialities were revealed to us in full. The sun had arched itself in such a way that it angled a strong beam down into the pit of the cavern. The bottom was strewn with papers, and these seemed to be covered with writing and printing.

"Love letters." "A mad book." "Drivel." "Lavatory paper."

In the middle of such speculation, Spark found himself facing another challenge.

"Dare you to go down there!" said Maps.

"Would if I could," sang Spark, assuming that any descent would be impossible.

At the start of our stay in Captain's Folly, these dares had been a way of our revelling in freedom. Behind all dares now was the hope that the result might involve some setback or embarrassment for the one challenged.

"Good!" snapped Maps.

Spark was immediately on guard.

"I'll getcha the rope," Maps went on.

"What rope? Where?"

"Jist over here."

Maps was already on his way to a miserable tree with its roots jammed into the rocks near the edge of the precipice. A length of rope was tied around the trunk and disappeared over the edge. It was knotted every two or three feet, like a decade from some crude outsize Rosary, and it had been used in the past by men who had climbed down to an ocean ledge to fish. Soft whiskers sprouted from it and trembled in the breeze.

Maps used his pocket-knife to hack the rope free. He

dragged it to another stunted tree, this one much nearer the hole in the rock, then wound it round the trunk several times and fed the loose end into the hole until it hung down inside from a peeling rock lip. He was well capable of having carefully plotted all that was to follow, but I cannot say whether he had been waiting on this chance or whether he had improvised on the spot.

"There y'are," he said, standing back and showing Spark the way down.

To anyone as unconscious of danger as Spark this was really no challenge at all. He was able to keep his feet against the rock wall inside the hole as he eased himself down knot by knot. When he reached the bottom the sound was like that of trampling in dry leaves but greatly magnified.

His voice reverberated. "Phew! Does it stink!" He picked up a sheet of paper and held it in the shaft of sunlight.

"What's on that?" demanded Maps, on his knees at the rim of the hole.

"Writin'."

"We know that! What's it say?"

"Come on down an' find out for yourself!"

Spark cocked his head into the shaft of sunlight and his eyes burned mockingly.

Maps shinned down the rope. I was next, then Fido. This sort of thing was difficult for Misty, but he was not long following, and soon all five of us were probing around in the papers and sneezing at the intense mustiness we stirred up.

Someone had suggested these were love letters. That was the closest guess, since we found stacks of letters, many in a foreign language, and sheaves of printed and hand-written music. There had been a fire here, but it had not touched the lower layers. And while it was different from having pine needles underfoot, it was a discovery that reminded me of the time we were in the island of pines and Double Martin began to reveal the truth about his past life.

We now peered into the past of Fingers Galore. Many of the letters were addressed to Seralius Hoffmann — his professional name — and they referred to concert engagements or formally returned his rejected musical compositions. We read the letters aloud in makeshift foreign accents, until we realised that we were probing into the shambles of a man's life. It seemed that Fingers Galore had dumped all his old papers here and set them alight, only to have the fire choke itself before the job was done.

Very casually, Maps moved to the dangling rope and said: "I'm goin' up for some fresh air."

No one stopped him. No one suspected him.

The higher he climbed, the less light entered the cavern, and he completely blocked it out momentarily as he climbed through the hole itself. Suddenly the rope snaked up after him.

At first we thought he was joking, and there was no fear in our demands for the return of the rope. Then we were chilled by a deep rumbling above us. It grew louder and louder, until a boulder — one of the rounded boulders cast up from the sea — fell into place in the hole and blocked out all the light except for some weak chinks around its edge. Heavy dust and flakes of rock fell on us and spattered on the carpet of papers.

Only when I remembered that I myself had imagined disposing of my four competitors was I ready to believe that Maps was really prepared to abandon us. Our shouted threats and pleas went unanswered. What was to stop him from returning to the McAnshes and telling them that we had been swept out to sea from the rocks?

In all my private enactments of the passing of Spark, Maps, Misty and Fido, I had encumbered myself with the bodies and staged a fine funeral in order to give myself the opportunity to indulge in some wet remorse. No such sentimentality could be expected from Maps. He would become Teresa's choice, Fearless' protege, as we rotted over the stinking remains of the lifetime failure of Fingers Galore.

Each of us tried to climb the rock wall to the hole, but without the rope it was impossible. Someone snivelled.

"Who's howlin'?" demanded Spark, though more in amusement than contempt.

No one owned up to it, and for some minutes there was only the dull thud of waves breaking on the headland, until the mild Misty vented himself on us: "You're all nuts, the lotta ya! Why don't ya ask Fearless which one it's gonna be, an' get it over an' done with?"

Misty had been the first to try to force a win for himself when he started weeding Teresa's garden. Now he was being the first to retire. In diplomatic terms this was the equivalent of stating that he had no further territorial ambitions — except that it seemed too late. Maps had buried us alive. Eternity would soon claim us. I could hear it booming louder and louder the longer I listened to those muffled waves.

Time can distort itself when minds are young and there is nothing to fill the eyes but darkness. Perhaps we were left for fifteen minutes in the cavern. Above us at last was a slight scraping. The boulder stirred in its seating, the chinks of light around its edges grew larger, and then it trundled away and the sun thrust its beam down onto our heads and the litter around our feet.

The rope was fed down, but there was no sign of any hands. All together *our* hands grabbed. We elbowed and shoved — like those wild kittens over a fish — to be first to climb up, until Spark shouted that the rope would break if we all tried together, and we slackened our holds so that he was able to take over alone. We allowed him to go, but Fido was starting at the bottom as Spark reached the surface, momentarily darkening the cavern again.

"Lemme go next," whispered Misty.

Even though I was still afraid of being trapped, I could not refuse him. However, there was no answer when Spark yelled at Maps to reveal his whereabouts, so I was able to take my time climbing out of what had threatened to be the charnel house of Captain's Folly.

Maps must have moved swiftly over that burred expanse of rock. Even with our hardened soles, we had to tread very carefully, so we had the consolation of knowing that Maps must have suffered some twinges to accomplish his disappearance. As we searched for him we had a competition, calling him everything from a two-faced schemer (Misty abstaining) to a two-legged rat, until the surface of the lake of lupins stirred as if a small shoal of fish had eddied. We found him there and he looked back straight-faced when we charged him with intent to dispose of us.

"Aw, I was jist givin' yer a bit of a scare, that's all," he blandly claimed.

Yellow and mauve lupin petals had fallen in his hair, but not even a glowing halo could ever give Maps Prior the necessary air of innocence. In discovering something about him, we had also found out something rather frightening about ourselves.

26 After that incident in the cavern, Misty was never quite whole-heartedly involved in trying to

win Teresa's approval, but Fido was still on the job out in the bay.

The tides and rough weather had restricted him in his attempts to beat Shellback O'Leary to the great prize that lurked there. We accepted it as inevitable that he would come to grips with the groper. It was one of those things bound to happen, like Spark becoming an auctioneer.

Of the storms that hindered him in his stalking, there was one that blew up violently in the night and battered around the sleeping-hut. We wrapped the distress signals closely about us, partly because of the unseasonable cold, partly perhaps because we were afraid the tumult might remind the flags of their pasts and incite them to take to the rooftops for old times' sake. All was calm by morning, yet when we stepped out we found the beach had been transformed.

"Crumbs! It's been snowin'!" cried Fido.

Between the sandhills and the tide mark were big white mounds. We had never seen snow. If any had fallen near St Roderick's the nuns would have taken it as a sign that the end of the world was close at hand. However, we all agreed with Fido. For a number of years we had been put to work by the nuns to turn out Christmas cards for generous patrons — the lanes of England decked out in snow — and this looked as if it might be the real thing.

Yet what we took for snow proved to be foam blown up by the storm. It was weightless, and turned to dirty water in our hands.

Some mornings after this we found Socrates the horse poised pensively over something that had been cast up from the sea.

Ambergris at last?

In that case, a mountain of it!

The previous evening, Fido had been out in the bay with heavy tackle and had played something big, so that Shellback once again resorted to banging the tyre-rim and yelling to Fingers Galore to help him warn his beloved quarry. To take the strain of the pull, Fido had wrapped the thick line around one of the canoe's outriggers. Line and outrigger had vanished, Fido very nearly capsizing. He paddled the crippled craft back to the rocks. We found him elated. No seaweed this time. He claimed he had played a really big fish. Yet we refused to admit that it could have been Henry the groper; that is, until we spotted the grey lump at the horse's feet in the morning. As we ran to it, that lump grew into the shape of a fish twice the size of the giant inland perch that had been taken out of the river some miles from St Roderick's. It was a tapering body attached to a huge head and mouth, and from its teeth a thick line wriggled over the wet sand down to the water.

"I got 'im! I got 'im after all!" whooped Fido with a warble worthy of Mrs McAnsh on a well-oiled Friday night, and the rest of us could have carried him out into the breakers and held him under until he gave up the gargle.

Fido began to dance around the fish as if his limbs were being jerked on invisible strings. Socrates backed away, possibly to protect himself from taking a bite. A fish this size could crack his teeth.

"How d'ya know he's a groper?" snarled Maps.

"With that big mouth?" said Fido. " 'Course 'e is!"

"He's not Henry."

"Gaw!" jeered Fido, giving us another version of a pint-sized scarecrow doing a war-dance.

"He ain't big enough."

"Fish don't look so big outa the water. You oughta know that."

"Watch him!" snapped Misty, getting behind his opaque spectacle pane as Fido knelt to peer into the glassy stare of the fish. "He could be still alive."

"Garn! 'E's the deadest fish ever you saw!" yelled Fido, jumping up, grabbing a twist of the line and giving it a yank. We scattered as the big fish quivered. "See! Whad-did I tell ya? 'E's dead. Dead as a doorstep."

Was this the same Fido who had been outstanding at St Roderick's for being so timid that the glint of an admonishment in the cold eye of a nun could make him freeze all over so that it seemed that a doctor who was also an expert safe-cracker would be needed to start him working again? The change was disgusting. He knelt and patted the monster.

"I gotcha, did'n I, eh? I gotcha!"

He was saying in effect that he had got himself well in line as Teresa's choice. He shook each of the rusted hooks embedded in the groper's jaws. This struck me as an affront to the creature's dignity. After all, by the standards of the fish world he was a distinguished inhabitant.

Fido's shouts and the sharp early morning echoes brought Teresa to the gap in the sandhills, just as Fido was rolling the groper over.

"There's barnacles on his belly!" Fido chanted. "He'd make a lovely jelly!"

Poetry now. Success had certainly transformed him. If he was destined to have a big head, we wished him one as impressively massive as that of the groper — and features as handsome!

Teresa was joined by Fearless, and they came down the beach together.

"I got 'im! I got 'im after all!"

Fearless wore a light robe that we had not seen before: black silk trimmed with orange, with *Fearless Foley* picked out across the back, also in orange. It dated from his days with the travelling show. The thought of Fido being free to wrap this around himself and stumble about in it made me feel even sicker. It was certainly not an image I would be mulling over in the picture-frame.

We received a grin all around from Fearless. He was tired, and we saw some grey in his tawny thatch of hair. He cocked his eyebrows respectfully as he looked down at Fido's victim.

"What have we got here?" he asked, going down on a knee.

" 'Enry the groper!" I said, pronouncing the name of the fish in Fido's style in honour of his great feat. I found myself moving in as stage manager. Fido would be in a position to invite a friend to stay under the Foley roof in coming holidays.

"It is him, too, by gum!" declared Fearless. He gave the belly of the groper a punch. It shivered coldly. Fearless grinned up at Fido. "You've made history."

"I reckoned it was 'Enry when I got 'im on the 'ook!" claimed Fido, starting the longest public speech of his life. He pointed to the ledge on the hillside on the south of the bay. "I went up there for days. I just watched. I worked out when 'e came outa his lair, an' all his 'abits. An' I got 'im!"

"What do you think of him?" said Fearless to Teresa, meaning Fido, of course.

"He's a born fisherman."

"Yeah, I suppose I am," Fido admitted readily, deciding that modesty and fame did not belong to each other.

Several of the weekend surf club men came down from the pavilion to admire the victim. Fearless examined the old hooks. "He was nearly nabbed a couple of times," he said, "but they didn't have your touch, Fido boy."

"No, they didn't, did they?"

Fido curled up his shoulders and preened, as if the words of praise were tickling him up and down the spine. In every male, however minute, there dwells a peacock.

Suddenly Teresa touched Fearless on the shoulder and whispered a warning. Before rising, he swivelled around on the balls of his feet. Others among us had already seen who was coming from the northern side of the bay: Shellback O'Leary, in flapping shorts and an old jersey, his legs grinding out a stiff pigeon-toed run. Slowly we moved aside so that no one would obstruct his view of what lay on the sand. He came to a stop twenty yards away and peered forward. Then he approached closer on the outer edges of his bare feet.

What had been a triumph for Fido, however deeply we begrudged it, was a tragedy for Shellback, and I tried not to look. Water was seeping into the hollows made by our feet in the wet sand. They were dwarfed by the marks of Fearless' feet, and the sight of them somehow signified to me that what was happening now belonged to the world of full-sized footprints. The old man's sense of loss conveyed itself acutely.

"Be the livin' Jesus," he whispered, "it cannot be himself. It cannot be Henry."

" 'Course it ain't!" cried Maps fiercely, to the perplexity of the adults. "He ain't anywhere near big enough."

"Yis," murmured Shellback, "perhaps that is so." He looked out to sea and let his eyes linger for some seconds beyond the waves, perhaps in the hope that if Henry were alive he would announce his presence with a dolphin leap. However, the surface did not break, and his eyes came back to the groper. "No, 'tis him for sure. Besides, me bones tell me so."

As Shellback went down on both knees beside the fish, a quick glance at Fido showed the first traces of dreadful misgivings.

"Well, Henry, there ye are now," he said. "After all the years I've bin stalkin' ye, here we are face to face at last." It seemed impossible that his voice could ever become so soft. His lips met without any trace of that explosive battering. "And what is this, in the name of hiven? An' this?" he added, discovering the old hooks, both embedded so deeply that the flesh had grown around them.

"It looks like someone else nearly beat you to him," said Fearless.

"Ah, yis," nodded Shellback, fingering one of the hooks. "I know all about this wun well enough. Henry wuz hooked — or so I'm told — be a fella who tried to step inta me shoes wunce while I wuz away in the city attendin' to the whereabouts av me pension money. Henry escaped, and this would be the hook that stayed, an' he's carried it around in his mouth all av five long years. This wun, though!"

He tugged the second hook, and as the groper gave a ghostly shiver Shellback treated us to a little of the fiery indignation we had come to expect from him. "This wun is a bronzed variety especially imported, and there's jist wun fella who had thim here in the Folly. After all this time I know him for the schemin' divil he wuz. He wint to the trouble av lecturin' me about what a great pity 'twould be if iver I wuz to hook and land a noble creature sich as Henry, yit he wuz sneakin' out at night himself." He gave a sharper tug on the hook that had retained some of its bronze finish despite the rust, and Henry seemed to affirm the allegation by giving a large wobble and shaking a fin. "Tryin' t'whisk the fish out av the ocean under me nostrils! An' this."

His voice became gentle again as he laid his trembling fingers with their striated tortoise-shell nails over a scar on the groper's side. "This would be the wound caused whan thim upstarts abandoned the fair rules av the game and tried to bring ye to reckonin' with a grenade smuggled back from the Great War."

Shellback rose and addressed us regarding the outcome of this piece of barbarity. "He came to the surface, his belly starin' up at the sky, an' I thought to meself thit he wuz done for. Smaller species were stunned dead for all time, but Henry was soon back to his sinses and swimmin' away. He wuz a great fish. The greatest ever I have known."

A wave fell. The seagulls clamoured hungrily as they circled above us.

"He's not the only pebble on the sand," said Teresa gently, while Fearless nodded heartily at her side.

"Ah, yis, but he wuz the only Henry in the sea."

At that moment I felt we had been badly mistaken about Shellback. He was no ancient ogre. He was a boy locked in a decrepit disguise. Some bloodshot membrane had grown over his eyes to mar the pure blue of a warm afternoon set in porcelain whiteness. All that leathery skin was a husk. His cragged hands were grotesque gloves that had grafted themselves onto him. Peel off the hide, the gloves, the membrane, and from that bald-headed cocoon would emerge a youth of milk whiteness with thick yellow hair matted like that of some new-born creature, so untouched by the sun that Teresa would go running for her bottle of sunburn lotion.

"I take it there'll not be any objections to a dacent burial for him?" came the meek request.

Fearless looked to the person who seemed to have the

strongest claim on the body, and with a frightened shake of his head Fido made it clear he would not object.

"Up the valley somewhere, perhaps," Fearless suggested. "We'll get the cart from the surf shed and wheel him wherever you want."

"Sweet Jasus," Shellback said to himself in a husky whisper, "now thit he's gone, what'll I be doin' with me nights and me days?"

Fido gave a whimper and turned and ran deep into the sandhills, even though Teresa and Fearless called after him to stop.

27

Another shadow fell over Captain's Folly that week-end: the shadow of St Roderick's.

Mrs McAnsh did not need to remind us that the date of our return was growing close. It was time, she said, for us to compose a letter to the Reverend Mother and tell her what a wonderful holiday we had been having.

It was always a grim shadow. Behind its high walls, St Roderick's was three stern storeys and a stifling attic. It was painted a drear battleship-grey and wore dull orange tiles fired from the clay that surrounded the town. It would remain our home for the next year. If by that time we had not been checked out to a new life with foster-parents we would be moved to another outback town and handed over to an Order of Brothers who would train us in farming.

Such was the future one of us hoped to avoid.

Spark was chosen to write the letter on behalf of the five of us. We were back from Mass in Serenity, minus the McAnshes. This time we understood their need of a drink. On the way over the hill they had been puzzled at how pebbles kept getting into our boots, thus requiring stops for us to empty them out, for we were all anxious that we should not arrive at the church in Serenity in time to go to Confession.

"Dear Fish-face . . ." Spark began.

"You're not gonna say that?" gasped Misty.

"Why not? That's what we call her."

While the rest of us found our exuberance increasingly stifled, Spark's spirits kept rising as sure as the high tides. This had a disturbing implication, of course. It could mean that he was not worried about the outcome. Privately, was he confident that he would be Teresa's choice?

He sat at the table in the McAnsh living-room, and he began to scrawl as he talked, as if dictating and writing at the same time. The first sentence went like this: "We were very sorry to hear that a mob of bullocks went mad in the saleyards and knocked over poor ole S'nt Roderick's . . ."

"Knocked it over?" cried Misty.

Even Fido was jolted. The news broke through the daze that had enveloped him since the incident that led to the burying of Henry the groper in the abandoned camp.

"Knocked it flat on its face ace-ace! All it is now is a dirty big pile of bricks. R.I.P., S'nt Roderick's!"

"You're kiddin'!"

"I'm not. I heard the wallop when it fell. Whirr-rum! Dum-diddle-dum! Woke me up." He scrawled on: "While it's gettin' stuck together again, we will be quite happy to put up with Captain's Folly. Besides, we have all got chicken-pox, mumps, measles, and a terruble catching disease —"

"We 'ave not!" Fido protested, as if afraid he might be put down like a sick sheep-dog.

"No? Look at me!" Spark coughed, spluttered,

sneezed, banged himself on the chest, reeled in a near faint almost off the chair, then more scrawl: "We might kill off everyone if we hurry back, so we will be very happy to spare you from affliction and stay on. I remain yours faithfully, the December boys." He made a mock flourish with the pen. "How's all that?"

"Spark," Misty assured him fervently, "we'll all end up with the backsides whacked out of our pyjama pants. The Reverend Mother will go berserk with the big strap."

"That don't worry me," said Spark. "Y'see, I don't think I'll be going back."

It was a taunt that stung Maps into action. "Let's just decide."

"Decide what tot-tot?"

" 'Oo stays."

Again the conflict that obsessed us flashed its ugliness in the open. What was Maps doing there at the doorway plucking grass-blades from beside the step? He came back, arranging them as if the middle of his clenched fist was some sort of vase.

"See what I got here: five bits of grass. They're not all as long as each other. We'll draw one each, see. Me, I'll take the one that's left. Whoever of us gets the longest piece is the winner, see."

With this, Maps thrust his fist and the tops of the five blades of grass at Fido. Freshly dazed, Fido was all set to oblige by taking the first bite at the bait.

"Steady on a tick!" said Spark quickly, without his chirp. "Maps knows which is the longest."

We could all believe this of Maps, although he denied it.

"I'll switch 'em around again," he said.

Behind his back he shuffled the blades of grass, then

brought his fist to the front with the tops of the green showing as before.

"Now I wouldn't know which is which," he claimed. "I ain't got eyes in the back of me head, have I?"

Fido was again invited to choose a blade.

"Don't be in it," warned Spark.

"I'm not gonna be," I said.

"Me neither," said Misty.

And now Fido withdrew his hand as if from something liable to sting him.

"Ya scared!" sneered Maps.

His offer was still refused, so he threw the five blades of grass to the floor. And now in a sober mood Spark composed a short, polite letter simply saying that we were having a wonderful time. He mentioned that we were tanned to the hue of the statue of the African saint in the church near St Roderick's. We had paid the nuns the compliment of wearing the bathing-costumes they had made for us until they were breaking out in holes. Next weekend Mr Tubby Porter was due to launch his boat. The weekend after this came the one big event of the year in Captain's Folly, the life-saving carnival. And then another weekend — fourteen days away — when we would be westward bound (four of us at least).

As for the wonderful time Spark mentioned, we had squandered much of it on jealousy and worry. Something had gone sour after the first two weeks. Was this due to some sinful weakness in each of us? Or were we to blame the advice of Father Scully? I felt that I should have taken some heed of the warning lying in the grass the day after the lupin-chase. Those withered petals: perhaps they had been trying to tell me that you had to take happiness as it came, and not ignore the present in the hope of something much greater in the future. Somehow our holiday was turning rotten, as those gleaming mauve and yellow petals had done.

28 A tidal-wave struck Captain's Folly during the following week.

Shellback had told us about the one that hit during the Depression, originating as a violent upheaval below the surface far out in the Pacific. It travelled as a sort of a shock wave. The hour of its arrival was predicted. The inhabitants of Captain's Folly — perhaps two hundred at the time — moved up the zigzag road. Right on time the water began to empty out of the bay, the prelude to the wave itself. It went out to a point far below the lowest tide ever seen, exposing rocks, slime, the mess of the sea-bed, all dominated by a heap of marine growth that was identified as the wrecked sailing ship. The water then swamped back, reaching the highest tide-mark, covering the concrete plaza in front of the surf club pavilion, threatening to invade the caves of Shellback and Fingers Galore. The sea flowed through the gap in the sandhills, but only to a level of a few inches.

My private tidal-wave — seen by courtesy of the picture-frame — formed a swirling lake behind the sand-hills. Teresa's shop was protected by a wall of sandbags. The sea entered Shellback's cave and left his fishing tackle in a tangle. Across the bay, it strummed a few dulled chords on the grand piano. When it sucked back — almost to the headlands — Spark, Maps, Misty and Fido started to run for the wreck, seeking plunder. They vanished into the hold through curtains of green and brown weed. Suddenly the sea roared in with the speed of the beam on Fearless' motor-bike, and the four of them were trapped and never seen again.

In this version of the disposal of my four rivals, I dispensed with the funeral. Teresa and Fearless were beside me the next day as I threw wreaths of sunflowers and ice-plant onto the water.

The greater my frustration at not being able to find any way to impress Teresa, the more elaborate the funerals.

29 As the tide went out next Sunday, Tubby Porter started his boat on its way to the sea. Wheels were fitted onto the cradle. The soft sand through the gap in the sandhills was no great problem. Flat boards were laid into a track, and Socrates was harnessed and called in to help. Teresa said it was the first work he had done since he pulled a plough for the men in the abandoned camp.

Tubby Porter wore only a pair of paint-stained khaki shorts. He shone like polished glass with sweat and had to keep brushing small showers of it from his eyebrows and his ginger moustache. (''He's like a water-bloomin'-fall,'' said Spark.)

Fearless was late joining the onlookers. He came out yawning heavily. There had been a strenuous morning of swimming and drill for the life-saving contests the following weekend, and he was exhausted after playing the important role of beltman. However, he soon stood by, regarding Tubby Porter's antics with a sort of wide-eyed delight, as if this might be the climax to a joke that the boat-builder had been hammering out for years.

A motor launch hovered out past the line of the breakers. It had a part to play in the final stage of the launching. The boat was brought to the shallow water. Socrates was released. The red and cream gloss of the hull was reflected like some distress signal fluttering with excitement. Now lines were passed either side of the bay to surf club men who kept the nose of the boat aimed at right-angles to the waves as the water rose under the cradle. Pieces of old car tyre were slipped between the hull and the cradle to prevent damage. Once the boat became sufficiently buoyant, it was hauled free.

There was no formal moment of launching, such as the smashing of a bottle of pumpkin wine over the boat's prow. Tubby Porter waded around to the side to climb up to the deck, and it was now that Shellback yelled at him from the beach: "Do ye know what ye're doin'?"

Tubby glared around like a startled pink frog. "I reckon so," he answered.

"Ye do, eh?" Shellback nodded to himself. "Well, all I kin say is ye're condemnin' yeself to an empty an' pointless sort av an existence."

"So help me! What are you rabbiting on about now?"

"How long have ye been workin' on the construction av this vessel?"

"Five years!" answered Tubby feelingly, as a small wave surged around his waist and and the boat bobbed heavily.

"Exactly. An' wunce ye've floated ye boat away out there, ye'll have nothin' to live for. Take an old friend's advice, Porter, and don't go ahead with ye plans. Now thit I've lost Henry, I know what I'm talkin' about."

"That'll be the day!" said Tubby after an incredulous stare at the source of the warning advice. "Don't worry about me. I'm getting this boat rigged down the coast, and then I'll be starting on my cruise."

"Ye better not count on me as ye navigator."

"Since when have I been countin' on you?" Amazement pushed aside the folds of fat around Tubby's eyes so that the blue glinted.

"Ye've bin droppin' hints enough," said Shellback. "Indade, if ivery hint wuz an empty beer-bottle I'd be up to me eyebrows in thim."

Tubby gasped for a moment, and then gave a laugh that would have been full of haughty disdain had he not been encumbered by a squeaky sort of voice. As he turned with the waves breaking over his belly and climbed on board his boat, he muttered something about Shellback's seafaring experience having been confined to the role of deck-hand on a coaling hulk in the city port. He signalled to the men in the launch. The main towing-line grew taut, and the new boat began to nose through the light surf. Fearless started three cheers for Tubby, and we joined in. And then, as the boat glided out past the breaking waves, Fingers Galore struck upon his grand piano.

We had not sighted him, but in honour of the launching he filled the bay with a majestic rendition of "Rule, Britannia".

30 It was about this time that we seemed to enter into an unspoken agreement to ease up on our waylaying of Teresa. We even went as far as avoiding too much of her company. We were all privately afraid that she might detect some of the evil emanating out of us as a consequence of our scheming. We had all made bids, however pathetic and feeble, to secure her exclusive patronage. Misty had remained distant from the conflict since the incident in the cavern, but he gave one

alarming twitch that had the rest of us believing that he was bound to be the winner.

We were high above the valley, using our pocket-knives to reshape the clay faces that had been carved there, removing the scabs caused by several years of exposure and making the eyes more Oriental. Suddenly Misty spun away from the clay wall and lifted off his spectacles. Something had given him a bad fright.

He squeezed his good eye shut. The useless eye was exposed for us to see, like boiled egg-white, the hazel of the pupil dimmed. We were frightened by this, but what he announced scared us even more: "I just seen somethin' outa me wonky eye."

To keep out all daylight from his good eye, he squeezed it tighter and pressed his palm over the socket.

"Whatcha seein'?" someone demanded.

"Lights," he whispered.

"Yeah?"

"Oo!" he murmured.

"Oo what?"

"Lights," he whispered again.

"What sorta blinkin' lights?"

"Swimmin' . . . beautiful . . . swimmin' all over the place . . ."

He was staring out over the valley, but he was privileged to see some wonderful sight to which the rest of us were blind. Any moment now he would see the Blessed Virgin floating in front of him. On this spot a cathedral would be erected. Misty Hayward would not only be adopted by Teresa and Fearless, he would also be canonised.

"What else?" pressed Maps.

"A sort of face . . ."

That was it! The Blessed Virgin!

Every move Misty made was followed by eight avid

eyes. He removed his hand, opened his good eye, then turned back to the clay faces. "It's only one of them," he said.

"Ya mean ya saw one of them mad faces outa your bung eye?"

Misty nodded dopily. " 'Tain't the first time it's happened. Outa me wonky eye I see things. First it's lights an' colours. An' then it's only somethin' I've seen with me good eye."

We were relieved, yet it did impress on us that things could happen in Captain's Folly over which we had no control.

"Is there anything wrong with you kids?"

In that same week, between the launching of Tubby Porter's boat and the life-saving carnival, Teresa caught us brooding on the sand. She looked to Spark for an answer.

" 'Course not," he said.

"You all look so sad."

We forced ourselves to smile.

"That's better. Perhaps you're homesick."

"Whaffor?" gasped Spark.

"Home."

"S'nt Roderick's?"

"Oh, dear," said Teresa hastily in the face of such incredulity. "Fearless isn't the only person who can put his foot into things. Cheer up. You're not back there yet. Think of all the fun you're going to have while I'm working next weekend."

"Workin', Miss, 'ow?"

"It's the biggest day of the year for the shop. I get swamped with customers."

She sat beside us and hugged her knees. She was

134

thinking. She became a little sad herself, as if something of our mood had been transferred to her.

Misty decided to try to cheer her up. "Miss," he said, "how about a cartwheel?"

"Oh no," she said quickly.

"You know," went on Misty, making a twirl with his forefinger. "One of them. A cartwheel."

"Yes, I know what you mean. But I don't think I should."

Misty was dismayed by this strange refusal, yet he felt he understood why. "Will it be all right tomorrow?" he said.

"What difference does that make, for goodness' sake?"

"Tomorrow's Friday. Don't you always feel like doin' cartwheels Friday?"

A smile at last. "That's right, Misty. Generally I do." Then she shook her head firmly and mystified us again. "But not this Friday. Not for lots of Fridays to come, perhaps."

No one ventured to ask why. No doubt we were all afraid that we might hear something that would shock or frighten us. What had entered into her life to make her so quiet and pensive? We watched worriedly as she looked around the bay. For a long time her eyes rested on Double Martin's garden before she referred to him in the same tender way as before.

"That poor man," she said. "He's so polite when he comes to the shop, although half the time he forgets what he came to buy. Often I have to run through just about every item in stock before I've prompted his memory. And sometimes I don't even do that." Once again she read off the despairing phrase about justice, and then went on: "I wonder what would happen if he woke one morning and found that it had been changed."

With the help of the picture-frame I had already toyed with the shells, rearranging them in a way I thought might appeal to Teresa, two lines of three words each:

GOD BLESS YOU
GOD BLESS YOU

Now Teresa decided exactly what she would like to see. "You could leave the top as it is, but change the bottom line. It's the same number of letters, too." She made a check with two fingers, counting on her bottom lip. "Well, almost the same number of letters. Just one word — 'tomorrow'." She then invited us to close our eyes and imagine the new legend in Double Martin's garden:

THERE IS
TOMORROW

Its meaning was as vague as the warning contained in those dying lupin petals in the grass, but I was conscious that she had changed the phrase from one full of despair to something containing hope. Among the five of us, as Teresa walked back to her shop, there was no discussion; but it was in our thoughts for the rest of the day. It was a challenge to each of us.

That evening in the McAnsh cottage we used pieces of *You Should Stop Your Vessel Instantly* and *I Require Medical Assistance* to dry the dishes. Later we lay under other distress signals. Everyone in the sleeping-hut was wide awake as a brassy moon began to glower outside. The flop and sizzle of the sea was like some marine monster snoring on the edge of the ocean, landlubbering for the night.

The first move was made simultaneously by Maps and Spark. They were on their feet, heading for the door, hissing their claims:

"Bags I the garden!" "I bags the garden!"

Misty, Fido and I were behind them as they scampered barefooted along to Double Martin's garden, the grey of their cotton pyjamas acting as a sort of undercoating for the slightly phosphorescent effect of the moonlight. They pushed and swiped at each other as they ran side by side, and when they reached the whitewashed stones that edged Double Martin's garden they began to fight, falling over the stones, scrunching around on the shells of the legend that had been worrying Teresa.

In this same week we had already witnessed one ugly fight. The kittens of the wild cat had grown, and they fought and made vile sounds at one another when Socrates delivered a fish to the rocks below them. It was not the fighting that shocked us so much as what we saw in those kittens: ourselves.

For fear of waking Double Martin, Maps and Spark did not mix in any threat or abuse with their punches, but those punches could be heard, and the ensuing grunts and winces and the crunching crack of the chalky shells under their feet.

They were not quiet enough. As Misty, Fido and I held back, we saw what the other two did not see: the head at the open window of the cottage. We started to back away, and at the same time the old man's voice wavered on the night air:

"Angels! My God, angels!"

Maps and Spark stopped struggling, and, Double Martin's voice growing thinner as he repeated his first cries, they joined us in a rush to the shadows of the trees so that we could sneak back to the sleeping-hut.

It was like a sharp nasty dream.

Yet next morning I soon saw it had been no dream. Maps and Spark had bruised knuckles and there were smears of blood on their faces. From the doorway we looked along to Double Martin's garden. During the night we had left the lettering broken up. Now there was no sign of a lone shell. It had been raked clean.

Later in the day Teresa came down the beach to speak to us. She was puzzled. She had served a customer shortly after daybreak. "Of all people," she said, "it was Mr Martin. He kept ringing the shop bell until I dragged myself out of bed to answer it."

He had wanted to buy flower seeds, and so Teresa was able to dispose of stock that had been on her shelves since the busy days of the Depression.

"He's a changed man!" she said, pointing to his garden. Double Martin had raked the despair out of it and planted the seeds of flowers, and they would bloom in the spring.

31 Early on the morning of the carnival, we quietly assembled beside Fearless as he stood watching the younger men anchoring red and orange buoys out past the breakers. He yawned in the middle of a big grin. "When do you pack up for home?" he asked.

"A week tomorrow," said Spark.

"That's what I reckoned. Ah, well, enjoy yourselves today. And next weekend I'll have a shot at getting even with you for the shock you gave me with all those road signs. It'll be the surprise of your lives!"

He left us in a mood of solemn contemplation as he

strode slowly up the beach and through the gap in the sandhills. We were sure we knew what the surprise would be: a joy and triumph for one of us, defeat and misery for the remaining four. Teresa had still given us no indication that she knew anything of Fearless' plan, but in a week she would be asked to make her choice.

An hour or so later the excitement began with a stately version of what Fearless presented as a wild solo performance on a Friday night. Down the zigzag road came a Highland band, the men all dressed in swinging kilts, boots and white gaiters, dark green jackets with silver buttons, and black and scarlet caps decorated with tartan ribbon.

In their wake came the competing surf teams and the visitors, by car, by bus and on foot. They parked themselves over the sandhills and up the valley. We regarded this as an invasion by foreigners. A hundred people darkened the surf at the one time. A large portion of the beach in front of the pavilion had been roped off as an arena for the land events and the start and finish of the swimming races and the rescue contests. We identified a few of the visitors as men who had resided in Captain's Folly during the Depression, and we followed them up to the abandoned camp. However, it was no sentimental homecoming.

"What a lousy dump this was!" said one.

"Yeah. I thought we were here to rot."

This certainly contradicted Shellback O'Leary's view that the Depression had been a time of good fellowship and nobility of the human spirit.

As the events of the day started, we were close to the roped arena. In the march-past, the pale-blue and yellow costume of Captain's Folly took its place with others, so that each of the seven teams became a sort of piece of walking heraldry behind the red-faced pipers of the Highland band. They did not shed their heavy uniforms, but kept to the shady side of the pavilion, a cluster of perspiring Tubby Porters. As the main event grew nearer — the one in which Fearless was due to swim as beltman for Captain's Folly — my misgivings about him increased. He seemed conscious of his own lethargy and disturbed by it.

My premonition of disaster must have been very strong. I slipped away to the sandhills, vacated by most of the picnicking visitors for the time, yet littered with their belongings, and I scraped the sand away and brought out the picture-frame. I was in need of protection, but this time the four sides could not rob the scene of its harsh reality. Long before Fearless reached the buoy where his team-mate waited to be rescued, he was in serious trouble. He was behind the beltmen of the other teams, his kick untidy, his overarm strokes irregular. As the linesmen hauled in the beltmen and the patients, the barracking on the beach grew louder and louder. Fearless and his patient were last by a long way, and when they came through the waves I wanted the picture-frame to black out the scene altogether, because Fearless was being supported by the man he was supposed to have rescued.

We had seen people collapse. There was the old nun who had slipped and fallen into a small moaning heap of black habit and Rosary beads on the floor I had polished too well in the main hall at St Roderick's. As we peered down into the saleyards from a high window, we had seen a marshalling hand run down by some bullocks and trampled. A silver-haired man had expired under the hot inland sun as the open-air congregation sang ''Faith of Our Fathers'' at the end of the procession on the feast of Corpus Christi. Yet we had never seen anyone as close to us as Fearless without the power to control himself. It was as if that war memorial Adonis at the crossroads had been struck by lightning, his foothold on the granite pedestal broken, so that he was teetering towards a fall.

Spark, Maps, Fido and Misty were opposite him at the roped arena, and I quickly reburied the picture-frame and ran down to join them.

Nearly all the strength had gone from Fearless' legs. He tried to straighten the kinks out of them as he was assisted to the hard sand, but the moment he attempted to walk alone he collapsed, and the thud came through the sand like the falling of one of the waves we called dumpers. He continued to spurn all help, knocking away the hands of those who tried to help him back to his feet. We would have gone to assist, except that a familiar voice growled behind us: "Hold hard, the lot av ye. There's enough of thim pesterin' the unfortunate fella without yeselves joinin' in."

Fearless pushed himself onto hands and knees and shook his head as if trying to rid himself of his weakness. A visitor — a man with bare feet, shirt hanging out over white slacks and a hank of black hair loose over one eye — knelt beside him and reasoned with him.

"Thit's Jimmy Sullivan," Shellback informed us. "He's wun av thim thit wuz here in the camp whan it wuz a place to be lived in." This merely served as an introduction to something nearer the O'Leary heart. "He's bin gone two years, he has, but he says he's niver forgotten Henry. He's shocked, I kin tell ye, t'hear thit he's with us no more!"

Sullivan gave up trying to persuade Fearless to let others help him, shrugged and rose and stood to one side. Fearless tensed himself for the effort of rising, his muscles taking shape and quivering, until suddenly he pushed himself upwards, swaying like a drunk and very nearly losing his balance again. He righted and steadied himself, and started up the sand. The life-saving teams were going through their drill under the eyes of the judges and marshals. Only six teams now. Captain's Folly had been forced to withdraw.

This in its way was the end of a reign. We sensed that. Yet it was one time when the sympathy of the young was on the side of the old dog. We were not surprised by Fearless' lapse. Teresa had prepared us by saying that he was past his best, and we had overheard some of the team members remarking that he was becoming slower through the water. I like to think that we were concerned for Fearless for his own sake, not for our own, not because any permanent injury might stop him from proceeding with his plan to adopt one of us.

He became shakier as the sand became softer. The rope was lowered for him, yet he still lifted his feet high over it. But the soft sand upset his balance again, and he fell once more, the fall cushioned. Now he was like a noble war memorial desecrated, the sand stuck to the wetness over his face and chest. Teresa came running to him through the gap in the sandhills. He tried to resist help even from her, but she tucked herself under his arm and supported him through the gaping carnival crowd and into the cottage entrance behind the shop.

"There's a tough cuss for you," said Jimmy Sullivan, and he seemed to us to be committing sacrilege by appearing amused. "Most characters I know would have been carried up there by stretcher."

"It wuz bound to happen," grunted Shellback.

"I'll see if I can help Teresa with some of those customers. They're piling up." Sullivan was tall and slim and long strides took him quickly to the shop.

Shellback turned away in disgust as there was a burst of cheering around the arena for the winner of the main contest of the day. We paid little attention to the result and took up a position in the sandhills to watch Fearless' bedroom.

The afternoon passed and the carnival came to an end. The stream of customers slackened and Teresa was able to slip through the house to Fearless, but he did not show himself. We began to ask ourselves how severe a shock he had suffered. Strange things could happen to people caught in the coils of the sea. Take Sister Agnes. I was always ready to believe that it was her near-drowning that had robbed her of the ability to laugh and enjoy life. Such might be Fearless' fate. And this was as terrible a tragedy as I could imagine for any man.

We kept up our watch and the sinking sun garbed the pipers in dark gold as they stood on the top of the hill and let their farewell lament mix in with the purple that already filled the valley. Most of the cars had gone by this time, all the buses. Only the litter remained, and a few couples locked together in the hollows of the sand-hills as the warmth seeped away.

In the past we had tormented courting couples by tossing roots of grass over sand-ridges onto them or by jolting the cars in which they cuddled. Tonight we were in no mood to be threatened or chased by irate Romeos. We were waiting for Fearless to rise again, but after visits from Jimmy Sullivan and other surf club men, both from the local and visiting teams, there was still no sign of him. The sand was cool under our feet as we went across and assembled outside the door. Nearby on its stand was the Red Indian motor-bike. It was more than just a vehicle to get Fearless from one place to another, it was a primitive musical instrument, like a man-carrying version of the bagpipes, and only an exceptionally audacious person could play it properly.

Spark was first spokesman when Teresa came to the

door, pale, her smile weak. "We're wondering how's Fearless?"

She shook her head sadly. "He just doesn't seem to understand what's happened to him."

"Does he need cheerin' up?" asked Misty.

"My word, he does!" Then she added quickly: "But he won't see anyone."

"Hasn't he heard any funny stories lately?" Misty persisted.

"He's in no mood for that, believe me!"

"But if he tried to tell one, he'd start laughing, wouldn't he?"

We understood now what sort of a cure Misty was prescribing. Yet he himself was already having misgivings. He shrank behind the opaque pane of his spectacles, tilting his head back a little, so that the pane caught some of the orange glow of the sunset and became a gold monocle stuck over his eye.

Again, Teresa shook her head. "No," she said. "That wouldn't work either. Not while he's in his present mood."

As she went inside, we turned away. The motor-bike had the air of being an instrument that might never again be played with the abandon of which it was capable.

Had the sea stolen Fearless' gift of laughter?

32 And had Teresa declined to do a cartwheel for us because she was saddened by some premonition of Fearless' failure?

These were questions we asked ourselves as we returned to the sandhills and watched the cottage at the rear of the shop, hoping for some glimpse of Fearless' shadow.

"Ho! Hullo there! How are we?"

It was Bandy McAnsh, and he was searching for us.

"Hah! There we are!" he said as we rose up on the ridge. He spoke a sort of weird reproving invocation over us. "Fingerprints, fingerprints, bottles an' dust! Upon my wretched soul, this is a merry little how-dee-do."

This would go down as a grim day for Captain's Folly. First of all Fearless had changed, and now that untrustworthy looking hat had turned Bandy's head at last.

"I'm warnin' you, lads," he went on, "my wife Mrs McAnsh is a mild an' lovin' person, all that a man can ask as regards a better half, but she's a very determined lady when she so desires, believe me truly." He doffed the headgear in question and the guilt began to flood into our nine eyes. "One moment I was in her bar, raisin' my hat an' about to order a drink, and before the effects had worn off I found myself flat-footed at a church altar. In her maiden days I have seen the same Mrs McAnsh perform extraordinary feats, and I have no reason to believe that she has lost her touch since the onset of matrimony. It so happens that I have seen her throw a man weighing fifteen stone out of her bar. Out! Into the street! What do you think of that, lads?"

We were thinking of that rigmarole he had uttered about fingerprints, bottles and dust. We were facing the fact that the mystery of the pumpkin wine had been solved. It was clear now that we had been identified as the alchemists who had turned Sundial Watson's pride and joy into cold tea.

"Ingratitude? No, lads, never. I highly enjoyed the proceeds of your purloining. As, indeed, did Mrs McAnsh herself. But now, lads — fingerprints, fingerprints, bottles and dust! — she's stalking about the cottage an' utterin' threats to have you hastened back to your Mother Exterior without further to-do. Everso, my lads, provided I can call upon your all-round agreement, I'll dispense the punishment." He patted his middle through his jacket, but we did not understand the significance of this. "Commit yourselves into my hands, and perhaps it will all blow over."

Commit ourselves into Bandy's hands?

Whatever happened, we felt that Captain's Folly now sported a fresh band of felons. We had been told by Shellback that the zigzag road had been built by convicts. We were already in chains, if it came to that, linked to one another by the fear that someone might slip away and pull off some stunt that would so dazzle Teresa that she would have no problem when called upon by Fearless to make her decision.

The arms that had flung fifteen stone of boozed manhood into the streets of Serenity were folded across a bosom athrob with indignant heavings.

"Here we are, Cynthia," said Bandy, as he ushered us into the McAnsh kitchen. It seemed unnecessary, but he counted us. "One — two — three — four — five. The full lot. I've rounded them up — all."

Mrs McAnsh gave a grim nod. Her mouth was puckered into a beak. We had never received a look like this without a starched wimple framing it. Like a big pepperpot, she began to shake out the outrage.

"Were I to tell her ladyship about this scandal, she would undoubtedly withdraw her generosity. But I would never dare expose her to such a dreadful shock, especially since she suffers from that weak heart condition. How many times you came in here and handed me and my husband a bottle of pumpkin wine with Mr

Watson's compliments, I hate to think. Why should you pilfer the wine? Would one of you care to inform me?"

Our only answer was a nervous scraping of bare feet on the linoleum floor.

"And as if what you'd done wasn't enough, you filled the empty bottles with cold tea and returned them to the shelves. Why?"

More sandy scraping.

"We might never have known anything whatsoever of this for some time to come, except that one of Mr Watson's visitors insisted upon looking into the mystery. He was not of the opinion that pumpkin wine could be turned into cold tea without any outside help. The fingerprints were discovered, and once Mr Watson and his friend came down here for a talk it was soon decided who was responsible. You might well have sent Mr Watson utterly out of his mind."

"Never fear," said Bandy, "they'll pay for it. All and one, they'll pay for it."

Had we been betrayed? He was unbuckling the belt around his middle. Only the monument erected by his wife's cooking stopped his trousers from slipping down and blinding the toes of his boots.

"Twelve strokes each!" Mrs McAnsh demanded. "Twelve of the best!"

"The very best," Bandy assured her, swinging the buckle of the belt towards the door. "To the sleeping-hut, lads," he ordered, but he winked, and a wing of his moustache twitched so violently that he might have been kicked on the right side under his chin.

As we slunk from the kitchen, through the living-room, and then across and into the sleeping-hut, we resigned ourselves to a thrashing that would make the efforts of the nuns at St Roderick's rate pretty feeble in comparison.

"Along now, lads," said Bandy, lining us up and jumbling his words expertly, "come and answer me up. Which of you is the one that's the best bawler of the lot?" He picked on me. "Start bawlin'!" he whispered, and began to replace the leather belt around his middle. "G'wan, bawl!" He waved his hand. "Twelve times."

Twelve wails to match twelve imaginary lashes with the belt, simply for the benefit of Mrs McAnsh's ears. I opened my mouth, but my affliction was back.

"Choker's all gummed up again!" said Maps in disgust.

"Then you try, lad," whispered Bandy. "Twelve heart-rendin' bawls. Get a start on!"

Maps wasted no time. He let out screams to chill the air of the summer night. With each scream, it seemed that the temperature of the valley must drop and that the ground would soon be twinkling with the hoar of a snap frost. Yet before he had reached the count of twelve, there was a rival scream from the cottage.

"Bandy, my love!"

"We done it, lads. We done the trick."

"Stop it now, Bandy! No more, no more!"

"Ah, the dear sweet creature. Heart of gold. Off with you, lads, while I look-see to the waterworks." He hitched up his trousers and headed for the sobs.

"You was good, Maps," said Misty admiringly.

"Aw, I was only gettin' tuned up," claimed the other as we left the sleeping-hut to continue our vigil in the sandhills.

The moon was coming up, and Teresa spotted us and called us over. We stood outside the cottage part of the converted railway carriage, near the open window where we believed Fearless was lying in a ferment of disgrace.

"Who was screaming?" she asked.

"Jist me," said Maps.

"Why? What was happening?"

"Mr McAnsh was supposed to be givin' me a wallopin'."

"How dare they ill-treat you!" In an instant she had become fiercely protective. "Fearless said it was impossible, but I wasn't so sure. I've never heard such screams."

"I reckon I can do worse 'uns," Maps assured her.

"There'll be no occasion for that. There'll be no more walloping. I'll see to that."

"It was only fun," said Maps, getting in fast just as Teresa seemed to be on her way to raze the McAnsh establishment.

"You call that fun?"

"Bandy wasn't hittin' us. He was just pretendin'," said Misty, sharpening the explanation.

"Just pretending? For goodness' sake!"

Fido took pity on her for her bewilderment. "'Is Missus ordered the 'idin', but 'e just kidded, an' Maps screamed 'is 'ead orf, and next she yelled out 'Stop!' Like 'e said, it done the trick. We're forgiven now."

"You're forgiven for what?"

"Pinchin' the pumpkin wine an' puttin' cold tea back into the bottles . . ." He petered out into a whispered "Crumbs!" as Teresa looked wonderingly from face to face.

"Naturally, Fearless and I heard something about Mr Watson's wine turning into cold tea," she said. "We thought it was just the poor man playing tricks on himself. Did you really do that?"

No one cared to admit anything, but Teresa extracted the story from us, starting from our plan to slow down Fearless. Between us we explained how we had to be free to erect the road signs and therefore have the McAnshes otherwise engaged. We told her how, for the sake of enjoying freedom at night, we had stolen further bottles, and of our qualms at the growing stack of empties and of the bright idea of filling them with cold tea and patching up the gaps on the shelves in Sundial's shed.

What we were careful not to tell was *why* we were so concerned in the first place to protect Fearless against himself. This might have been wheedled out of us but for the alarming sounds that came from the open window opposite us: snort, groan, sob, hiccough, moan, wheeze, howl, all in quick succession from the same source. It reminded us of the sheep-dog dying in whimpering agony in the saleyards after being kicked by one of a bunch of wild camels, or the woman who drunkenly wept for her sins outside the convent wall on Friday and Saturday nights.

"It's only Fearless," said Teresa, aware of our terror.

"Quick, miss!" cried Fido. "''E's takin' a fit!" He was partly correct.

Fearless loomed in the open window, shuddering, shaking, pressing tightly overlaid palms into his stomach. We were horrified, until suddenly, like the explosion of the Red Indian motor-bike when the starter was kicked, he let loose a blast of laughter. His hands came away from his middle and he grasped the window-sill and weaved around helplessly as the laughter streamed from him. A whole dam of it had burst asunder.

What we had done now dawned on us, and we began to laugh with him. It was as if we had pinched all that wine not to protect him from his impetuosity, but to free him from a curse when the time came.

33 "Boy, I sure would like to have a shot at auctioning off this lot!" said Spark, eyeing the ornate clutter in the sitting-room of Lady Hodge's mansion.

Mrs McAnsh borrowed a gasp and a phrase from Bandy: "Upon my wretched soul!"

Surprise was in the air already. As we waited for our last weekend and Fearless' promise, Mrs McAnsh sprang one on us: the threatened visit to our benefactress. But *her* surprise was to find Spark in the mood to empty the mansion of its treasures and fittings. Bronze angels and marble lovers, a delicate tapestry showing St George lancing a dragon the size of the late Henry the groper, many murky wall paintings of oil and water colour, vases, dishes with pictures in them, bowls, paperweights, chandeliers, brass fireside tools, stuffed velvet cats with red and emerald glass buttons for eyes, furniture covered with flower-pattern material like thin carpet, and a carpet underfoot that was a conglomeration of urns and roses.

It was mid-week, but we were back in Sunday boots, together with serge shorts, white shirts and ties. We were expected to be duly overawed by the surroundings after being let through the wall gate by her ladyship's housekeeper and then led through a break in a barricade of barbed wire that was overgrown with creepers. All of us were able to oblige Mrs McAnsh in this regard — except Spark. He found himself confronted with enough raw material for auctioning to raise the debt on St Roderick's and build the new wing. One of us just needed to whisper a bid and he would have been off, despite the strength of the starch in the eyes of Bandy's beloved.

The occasion was represented to us by her as a treat and an honour. Not only would we meet the generous titled lady who had not as yet been sighted by us, but Father Scully was coming to say Mass on the premises. We were informed — in a suitably hushed way — that Lady Hodge had not been out of her house since the passing of her husband, and that had been before the end of the Depression. We were no great distance away from the lake of lupins, but we had been ushered into another world. I was conscious of various nervous twitchings by Fido from his ankles to the top of his head. Misty was giving the place the once-over around the edge of the opaque spectacle pane. Maps had his top lip cocked up slightly, a sign that he was reasonably impressed.

The housekeeper was the thin, sallow woman we had seen dusting the grass with a dog that looked as if it ran along on ball-bearings. She helped the tiny widow of Brigadier-General Sir Henry Hodge into the room, and Mrs McAnsh glared us up onto our feet.

Lace and this little old lady are always linked in my mind. Despite the drabness of our lives at St Roderick's, we had regular dealings with lace, and lace of the most ornate types. The priest's chasuble was a beautiful garment, thanks to so much lace. The surplices we wore when taking our turns as altar boys were trimmed with it at the elbows and around the thighs. Much of it was woven on the spot in the workrooms at St Roderick's. Lady Hodge wore a long dress of grey linen. All the forearms seemed to be covered with fine lace. There was more of it down the front, and a knot of it was held by a gold pin under a shrunken chin. Her hair was very white, and her eyes wavered like the bubbles in the spirit-level that we had seen among the tools used by Tubby Porter.

Mrs McAnsh took her hand and kissed a diamond ring as if Lady Hodge were a female bishop. Her ladyship peered past her and leaned her head to one side and treated us to an exquisitely charming old-world smile. "Ah," she breathed by way of a greeting.

By her own actions Mrs McAnsh instructed us to throw our shoulders back and smile in return, and she gave a nod of approval when she saw that we caught on to her meaning.

Lady Hodge kept peering and smiling. "Are they not all girls?" she inquired sweetly.

"Dear me, no, your ladyship, they're not all girls," Mrs McAnsh hastened to explain.

"Boys, my lady," put in the housekeeper, fitting lorgnettes into the old woman's hand and helping her lift them before her eyes. "Last year's lot were girls," she said. "These are all boys."

"Oh, yes, yes, so they are. Boys!"

"Fine lads if I may say so, your ladyship," Mrs McAnsh informed her, despite the pumpkin wine. "So very handy and helpful around the house."

"Such pretty boys," said the titled lady.

There was no need to glance at any of the others to know that I would find them stunned with dismay at this. Pretty boys, indeed! What had that sunburn lotion done to us?

"I cannot tell you how long it is since I saw a boy," went on Lady Hodge, and when she uttered the word "boy" she seemed to make it burst apart, as if she had a smear of Shellback O'Leary's explosive moistness on her lips for this one word. "No, I don't believe there has been a boy here since my son. Stella," she said to the housekeeper, "whatever did become of him?"

"Your son, my lady?"

"Yes, Stella, such a sweet boy."

"Mr Francis passed on last year, my lady."

"Did he really?"

"Yes, my lady."

"What a pity. A very great pity."

She beamed back at us, and I felt she would have remained smiling innocently even if we had all dropped dead at her patent-leather slippers.

"Have you been enjoying a pleasant holiday?" She asked.

"Dear me, yes," Mrs McAnsh assured her on our behalf. "Thanks to your wonderful generosity, your ladyship, it has been a time of utter contentment for them."

"I am so glad." She spoke on to us. "You'll find this a peaceful place nowadays, but in Sir Henry's time it was an armed camp. We lived in mortal dread of our lives, you know. Stella, do take the young gentlemen up to Sir Henry's seclusion room. It is still there, I suppose?"

"Oh, yes, my lady."

"Do take them up there, Stella." And then as the housekeeper led us out of the room, she added to Mrs McAnsh: "They are such pretty boys . . ."

We were intrigued by this strange little woman, yet pleased to escape from that insulting compliment. She was odd, but I could not quite imagine her obliging Shellback O'Leary's fancy and lighting candles for the dead with five-pound notes. The talk of the valley being an armed camp gave us the first glimmering of a reason for that barbed wire inside the wall. We followed the housekeeper up stairs completely carpeted, and I noted that here was another knobbly pair of ankles that looked as if they had some nuts that needed tightening. As we climbed, statues with empty eye-sockets loomed over us, together with portraits of stern gentlemen who seemed to be on the verge of belching and ladies with wreaths and nightcaps on their heads. Here was opulence dating from a time when the valley below was full of men starving from lack of food and hope, its incongruity and injustice apparent to us. We came to a spiral stairway of iron and the housekeeper told us to go the rest of the way on our own, and so we clanged up in our boots.

The heat of the glassed-in room and the stale air hit us before we reached the top of these noisy stairs. We began to perspire immediately. The eight windows that made an octagon of glass were dusty on both sides. Spiders' webs were abandoned and the husks of their former residents lay with dead flies and moths on the inside ledges.

The view was no better than we had secured many times from the zigzag road, but it was infinitely more exciting, as we seemed to be inside an eye of a sort. The heat was fierce, making it a very hot eye, but suddenly we were frozen by a dry creaking sound over our heads.

Eeee . . . eeek . . .

We all looked up to the ceiling of painted wood. It put our teeth on edge. It was as if some horny reptillian creature were trying to scrape its way inside.

Eeee . . . eeek . . .

"Aw, it's only that arrow thing up top," Maps decided, meaning the gilded weather-vane.

On the ledges were two sets of binoculars and a brass and leather-covered telescope. Maps grabbed the telescope, and Spark and I claimed a set of binoculars each. We had to wipe the dust away from the glass at either end before we could start trying to focus. Misty consoled himself with a mirror, dusting it across the seat of his pants and then catching the sun in it and aiming the reflection at the hillside opposite, making a bright blob of light race up to the vague shapes of the clay faces and flash down to the water where Socrates stood up to his fetlocks. The blob shimmered on the surface, and Misty squealed with glee as the horse feinted at it, as if it were some ghostly fish.

A sedan car upset our antics. It came down the zigzag road to our right, and then drove across and stopped outside Teresa's shop. I tried to focus on it, and so did Maps and Spark, but we had yet to capture a sharp image of anything.

Fido switched our attention back into the tiny room itself by growing excited at some discovery on the round table set in the middle. There was a diagram on it, which he claimed was a map of the valley. We only accepted this when our expert, Maps, nodded agreement.

The camp that now lay abandoned was clearly marked, every path and hut outlined. Under this was printed the wording: *Disposal of Enemy Forces*. The diagram now became a military plan. We sifted through papers and found neatly-written sheets entitled *Orders of the Day, Battle Plan* and *Password Key*. On this last sheet were words such as *Evanescent,* and phrases such as *The Duck is Yellow* and *The Flamingo is Ripe*. It gave us a picture of the late Sir Henry and what had occupied him during his retirement.

"He musta had a hit on the head, too," commented Misty, as if he had unearthed another victim from the time it rained flower-pots over Captain's Folly.

The small garden at the rear of the combined shop and cottage was the target for the binoculars and telescope. Maps was first to focus clearly. He twitched into a tense attitude and then hissed slowly before uttering words deeply charged with shock and loathing: "The dirty dog!"

Although my image was still blurred, I realised what Maps meant. In that square of lawn hemmed in by a windbreaker of high bushes and trimmed poplars, a man had joined Teresa. He stood with his arm around her waist and then led her to a garden seat and settled into it beside her, holding her hands on his knee.

"That's that fella Jimmy Sullivan," said Spark.

Near them was a small apricot tree sprinkled with red-gold fruit. I had the feeling that this intruder might reach for an apricot and tempt Teresa to a bite. Old Nick had hovered around Captain's Folly since our arrival, and now he was the serpent in human form.

In this initial stage of shock we refused to entertain the possibility that Teresa was being disloyal to Fearless. We united against a common threat, the worst and most terrifying threat so far. Our belief in the goodness of Teresa and the exclusiveness of her devotion to Fearless had become stronger than our belief in the existence of God.

Unknown to us, had something been happening between Teresa and Jimmy Sullivan? We recalled how on the previous Sunday, Sullivan had hastened to help Teresa. Did this explain why she had not been in the mood to do any cartwheels?

"Boys!"

At least the housekeeper had our sex right. She called from the bottom of the iron stairs, and we descended right down to the ground floor to be led into a larger room, where Father Scully was already attired in vestments, wearing the green that indicated this was an ordinary day of the Church, in contrast to the white and gold of the feast days, the red for the martyrs and the black for the dead. A table was covered with a white cloth and became the altar. Bandy McAnsh was bareheaded and ready to be the oldest acolyte we had ever seen in action. Once the Mass began, he mumbled his Latin responses so quietly that we could not decide whether he was distorting them or not. Mrs McAnsh knelt primly and ran her Rosary beads through her fingers as if getting in some extra prayer on the side. Lady Hodge remained seated throughout the periods of kneeling, standing and sitting, in a chair with a high back like the facade of a Spanish church in another of the pictures in the visitors' room at St Roderick's. Her housekeeper knelt beside her and only moved away once — to collect the dog when it began to sniff around Bandy's boots.

Father Scully beamed with shut eyes as he turned towards this privileged congregation to bestow the blessings. I felt that he might have been unable to smile — in fact, that he might not even have been here — but for the way that we had delayed a recent Sunday morning arrival at his church so that we would not be in time to go to Confession. If we had owned up to all our scheming and murderous intent, he might have fled from his box. Yet I could not regard that special penance he had given me as a mistake. It was beginning to have a purpose.

As the priest went through the ancient ritual, we were five worshippers in body but not in mind. We were occupied in thinking about the two mortal beings we worshipped. I was scanning the past from the morning of that first dazzling cartwheel to find something that might explain why Jimmy Sullivan and Teresa should be on such intimate terms. Shellback had told us that this man had been in Captain's Folly during the Depression. Perhaps their special relationship went back to that time.

However much I thought around the matter, I kept coming back to what I was afraid to face: Fearless was being betrayed by the very person who should honour him most. Yet I could not bring myself to allow one whisper of guilt to be associated with Teresa, even within my own mind. If there was anyone to blame, then all the blame originated with this Jimmy Sullivan and lay with him.

We believed Teresa and Fearless to be two people satisfied with their lot. The Depression had robbed everyday life of much of its luxury, so that the simpler things had come to be valued and enjoyed. It was a time when faith in human goodness — despite all the evidence throughout the world to persuade people to the contrary — was still widely held, a time when kindness was not necessarily regarded as a weakness or something to compensate for pangs of conscience brought about by evil done or evil merely thought. We had not seen or heard anything to lead us to think that either Teresa or Fearless was unhappy. It is true that Teresa had once disturbed us by expressing an interest in the escapist part of convent life, but then she had laughed at herself and we had accepted it as no more than a whim. Many times we had heard her say proud and loving things about Fearless. And even if we had never actually heard the equivalent from him, we had seen it in his eyes. He did not need words when he could express his devotion by way of a rocketing motor-bike. Friday night's joy was so intense that we could not help but share it, even though we were petrified for the duration of Fearless' plunge down the zigzag. When he arrived and took Teresa into his arms, it was to us as joyous an occasion as human beings were capable of experiencing.

"Oh, they'll be so beautiful when they grow up, I'm very sure," said Lady Hodge to Mrs McAnsh. The old lady was apparently thinking we were girls again, but that did not upset us now. We were desperate to be set free to try to find out the extent of the calamity that had disclosed itself to us near that small apricot tree. We were frantic. Misty showed one haunted eye. Maps' face was pinched more acutely than ever. Fido was in such a fidget that his hands roved around not knowing where to scratch.

"They'll never forget you, your ladyship," quavered Mrs McAnsh, moving herself to the brink of tears. "As long as they live, they will never forget you."

With a moist cocking of her eyeballs Mrs McAnsh gave us the signal to agree with her, and we muttered our thanks awkwardly.

At last we were released into what had been enemy territory to the late Sir Henry, only to be halted on the narrow path and jeered at by the sound of the sedan starting up the zigzag in low gear. And to taunt us even further, we glimpsed Teresa waving good-bye from the front of the shop.

Usually we would have tugged off our boots and set our feet free, but there was no time for that. We ran across to the shop and we were shocked again. Teresa was singing.

34 Death stalked yet again within the four sides of the picture-frame.

Once I was back in my bathing-costume, more skin showing since the rooster emblem had lost its tail and another hole had robbed *Excelsior Flour* of several letters, I managed to slip off alone long enough to take out my special treasure and look through it. Maps and the others had satisfied themselves that it was unlikely to prove to be a passport to Teresa's affections, although they were amused and scornful at my attachment to it.

("You'll end up with a beaut pair of square eyes!"
Spark warned.)

This was the window through which I had watched
some of nature's living abstractions: the drift of clouds,
the coruscations of a sunset, the dance of light as the
wind shimmered a hillside of polished grass. Through it
I had made many bids to install myself as Teresa's
favourite. I had marched as standard-bearer for the
Captain's Folly Surf and Life-saving Team, yet the ban-
ner did not say this. It said something much more
important. It was scarlet silk emblazoned in fresh gold
braid with the words *Fearless Forever*. I had seen myself
as a multiple cartwheel expert flashing across the sand. I
was the smallest rider who had ever marked that same
stretch of sand with figures of eight on a Red Indian
motor-bike. And since Teresa herself had seen some of
my finger-painting in the abandoned camp and suggested that one day I might be an artist, I had filled that
frame with some portraits of her and Fearless.

Now as I lay within hearing of Teresa's singing as she
moved about the cottage and shop, I put Jimmy
Sullivan in the picture-frame. He had decided to come
back, according to my version, and he was out to
impress Teresa by streaking down the zigzag with the
abandon of a Fearless Foley. He did not have the touch.
The first hairpin bend trapped him. Over he went, the
sedan car bouncing, throwing off mudguards, roof,
radiator, wheels, spare tyre, and joining them in
vanishing under the surface. Sullivan came up gasping
and splashing, only to be menaced by the first school of
sharks ever seen in the bay. They carved up the water
around him, as if they were performers in some marine
Wall of Death. I stopped short of allowing them to
make a meal of him. Fright and exhaustion killed him.

With a wail he went under for the first time, the second time, the third time. Then he was gone.

Having disposed of this threat to the harmony between Fearless and Teresa, I changed the picture.

The frame again became an instrument of death, the doorway to an inferno. My imagination, stoked with anxiety and frustration, might almost have set the wood itself alight. Spark, Maps, Misty and Fido coincided a visit to the abandoned camp with the spontaneous combustion of the hidden store of fireworks. They were blown apart in a geyser of smoke and flame.

Yet what use was it to dream of outright triumph now? If Teresa and Fearless were to be estranged, there was hope for no one. The combination of Teresa and Jimmy Sullivan did not allow for the presence of any one of us.

35 Now that we could no longer use an inquiry about the groper to open the conversation, it took time to get Shellback started up. We had to survive a series of grunts and cold suspicious glares in answer to our prodding questions. I still had the feeling that a bewildered boy dwelt in that wrinkled cocoon.

Maps began the lead-up to the question of the day that afternoon. "That man you said was called Jimmy Sullivan came back here this morning."

"Did he now?" said Shellback softly.

"It was when we were up to meet Lady Hodge."

"She's a kindly soul."

"We climbed right up to the turret, to Sir Henry's seclusion room."

"Yis, he wuz a great wun for bein' on his own."

"We reckon he was touched," said Spark.

"Touched?"

"A bit," persisted Spark, tapping his forehead.

"Who is to judge?" murmured Shellback with a shrug.

"Mister O'Leary," put in Misty, "now we know how your groper got its name."

"Ye do?" said Shellback, livening it with sharpness.

"You called him after Sir Henry," said Misty, before realising, to his dismay, that he was speaking of the dear departed.

"I've wondered about that meself," Shellback mused. "No, it wuz merely the first name thit came inta me head, an' he might jist as well have bin Tom, Dick, or Mad Harry. Yit 'tis possible thit in me unconscious mind I wuz mebbe payin' Sir Henry an honour. Yis, mebbe that wuz how it happened."

"What sort of a fella is Jimmy Sullivan?" inquired Spark, coming back to what Maps had started.

"We've none av his kind here these days," said Shellback, making him neither good nor bad. He did not allow us to follow up our question. "I don't suppose the time of ye goin' back is too far off now, eh?"

Spark admitted this for all of us. Just a few days.

"Ah, well, ye'll be leavin', I trust, with somethin' learnt t'help ye through the pitfalls av life." He indulged in one of the few smirks we had seen from him since the passing of Henry. "I'm told ye brought ole Watson to a realisation of what it might be like t'find the hand av God workin' miracles in y' back shed. Tis a pity ye've not bin able t'make iny impression on thit menace across the bay. He's a broken man, he is. His whole concert career wint up in smoke, an' I suppose he's blamin' the Depression like the rist av thim did. They were days the like av which we'll never see again." Suddenly he eyed us as if he had made a discovery. "There's only four av ye!"

"Fido's in the sandhills," someone explained, letting Shellback judge the reason for this absence himself.

"Ah yis, we know Fido, don't we? Nevertheless, I might have news for that young desperado before ye leave. I might have some great news for him."

This sent a shiver of dismay through us. Fearless had told Shellback of his plans for one of us soon after the midnight rescue on New Year's Eve. This might mean that Fearless had already intimated to Shellback who was most likely to be Teresa's choice. Perhaps the landing of Henry was not such a mistake after all.

We drifted back to the sandhills.

However, no one had to resort to a blunt question: it was apparent that Fido had no idea of what Shellback might have been hinting at. Still, he needed watching, and so long as he stayed in the sandhills we remained with him.

Teresa came to the door and shook out a small tablecloth and waited for the birds to swoop in for the crumbs. We ducked down behind a ridge topped with tussocks. We had been taught to differentiate between two main types of sin — venial and mortal. By being disloyal to Fearless, Teresa might be guilty of mortal sin; that is, if we admitted any disloyalty, which we did not. Yet the situation could be even worse — if Teresa was being disloyal and at the same time happy about it, that would be something that had been described to us as sacrilege, like a deliberate desecration of a church. She turned back inside and began to sing again. I wanted to jam my hands over my ears. Of all songs it had to be "I'm Painting the Clouds with Sunshine".

The kittens — soon due to be called cats — brawled

among themselves, clawing at one another, somehow defacing the beauty of the day. We wandered up the valley in search of diversion. The sun was strong enough for the ice-plant tapestries to be showing their most brilliant hues, but the gloss was peeling away from the blooms. In the abandoned camp the big sunflowers stood with heads dropping as if exhausted after long spells of sentry duty. We had seen two full moons over Serenity during our stay here, and now there was a daytime moon, a thin shred of white fingernail floating in the sky.

Back we came to the sandhills, and Teresa was still singing.

It was impossible now to suppress the feeling that our machinations against one another might have brought about this threat of disaster to the lives of Fearless and Teresa. It made a mockery of all our fine notions about what our fathers had been: mine a painter, Spark's an auctioneer, Maps' a secret service agent, Fido's a fisherman, and Misty's — like his mother — a person with beautiful eyes. We were surely the abandoned sons of hardened criminals.

Through the hot sand came the clump of the waves, and then from behind the hills to the south of the bay came a sound that made us curl up onto our knees to listen better. A sound we had heard only by night could be different by day, yet that dull growl, audible only for a moment, reminded us of the one that had heralded Fearless' arrival on the Red Indian motor-bike. When the wind was behind him, the sound of the engine often carried well ahead. A second growl was longer, and it started that live duster yapping behind Lady Hodge's garden wall. Could this be Fearless hurtling home by daylight after having heard of Jimmy Sullivan's visit?

Within half a minute a motor-bike did pause at the

start of the first downward leg of the zigzag, but the machine seemed too small for the Red Indian and the man astride it could not be immediately identified as Fearless Foley. He was without helmet, without leather coat or leggings. Yet when the descent began, with a booted foot going out at each turn and a cockade of dust kicking up at the rear, we knew it was our male idol, and, even though this was the first arrival we had seen without the swinging and vibrating beam of the headlamp, the sight of him manhandling that iron mount more than compensated.

We were on our feet now. Teresa had appeared at the door as the Red Indian proclaimed Fearless' presence, but she vanished inside and there was no sign of her as he skidded side-on to a stop near the paling fence. The engine cut out, and he quickly set the rear wheel on its stand and ran into the cottage.

It was impossible to look at the others. I was afraid of the dread I would see in their eyes. In the past we had happily interpreted the noise of his explosive arrivals as high spirits. This time it might be a measure of his righteous anger. We heard him yell inside the cottage, and took this as confirmation of our misgivings.

Consequently, we were baffled when he came charging out, the goggles still on his face. He ran in great loping strides through the gap in the sandhills, until he came to the plaza in front of the surf club pavilion. A running jump took him onto the concrete, and in a few strides he had grasped the alarm rope and started the bell clanging wildly.

It brought Shellback to his ledge on one side of the bay, and Fingers Galore to his on the other side. Teresa followed at an easy jabbing walk over the sand. While Fearless was on his way down the hillside, she had slipped on a fresh frock. Maps started to run, and we all followed. Shellback was coming too.

Our bewilderment increased as we found Fearless grimed and in working slacks and shirt, as if he had come straight from the tunnel face. Now he pushed the goggles up onto his forehead, leaving red marks under his eyes, and also the outline of dust.

As he let the rope dangle, the bell stopped and he took a deep breath. But then he seemed overcome with shyness. He waited until Teresa joined him on the plaza, and to our amazement she showed no guilt, no fear of any drastic action Fearless might be contemplating. In fact, she carried herself with a wonderful air of contentment.

"Hey!" cried Fearless. "I seem to be carrying on like a raving nut-case!"

"You sure are!" she laughed.

He took another breath as we held ours. "I've got something I want to make public," he said, and he might have been the war memorial Adonis finding the power of speech after years of silent sentry duty. He waved over his shoulder up the valley. "After last Sunday I felt I was finished. I thought I was ready for the rubbish-dump. And, now, well, my wife's been keeping a secret from me." He grinned at Teresa, and we all quaked as we steeled ourselves to hear the announcement of the candidate for adoption. "It *is* true?" he asked.

"Fearless, darling, Jimmy Sullivan's positive — and he knows about these things."

How had that fellow become involved?

"In that case," went on Fearless, scratching deep in hair dusted by his fast ride on roads with loose surfaces, "the impossible seems to have happened. Some poor kid is going to have to put up with me. It's true, so help me, you heard my wife say so. She's going to have a baby.''

In our time at Captain's Folly, we had stood side by side as variations on many themes, but surely we had never been able to present utter dumbfoundedness so brilliantly, so completely, so exquisitely as now.

"Isn't it great news?" he enthused, looking to us.

Only Maps was capable of making any noise. He gulped loudly. It sounded like a plug being pulled out.

Teresa looked at him, and then at each of us: five blank faces. Her eyebrows came closer to form a faintly puzzled furrow. It was almost as if she were on the brink of discerning what had accounted for our odd and fevered behaviour in the preceding weeks.

"You know something?" she said thoughtfully, "I'm inclined to blame you boys for what's happened."

Fearless gave a strangely horrified squeak and leaned away from us and gaped questioningly at Teresa.

"I'm serious. On that first day the boys arrived here, I felt that it was time we had someone of our own."

My eyes were slightly out of focus, my ears felt thick. All in one I might have received a whack on the nose, a cuff on the ear, a dumping from a rogue wave and a boot in the backside. It reminded me of the time of our first dip in the sea when we staggered out with water caught in the bottom of our newly christened bathing-costumes. We were left flat-footed and fooled. Yet we had fooled ourselves this time. Fearless had meant well when he spoke of adopting one of us, but it was the same as Teresa thinking she might like to escape into a convent. We had done the rest. We had brought this twist upon ourselves. We had wasted weeks of freedom. More clearly than ever I had an understanding of the warning contained in those lupin petals as they lay withering in the grass. And while we knew now why

Teresa was wary about performing cartwheels, one point still puzzled us, and Fido timidly put the question: " 'Ow does Jimmy Sullivan know?"

"He's a doctor."

Ah, of course. He would be one of the men of learning who had been marooned here during the Depression.

"I spoke to him last Sunday. He said he'd come back to see me."

"He phoned the works' office and left a message," said Fearless. "Blow me down! At my time of life."

We tried to grin back at him, but it was taking us time to unlock. We were a foolish fivesome in danger of being turned into statues, perhaps to stand here as a warning to succeeding holiday guests of the McAnshes not to seek more than Captain's Folly could offer. Spark was the first to break loose. He began to swagger around and warm himself up, his chirp back again.

"Hurrum! Hoo! Hee! Haw! . . ."

36 Fearless had promised us a surprise, but his announcement was not it. The next Saturday afternoon, our last in Captain's Folly, he took care to be with us when, like a motor-bike throbbing in the sky, a silver biplane banked over the bay.

"There he goes!" Fearless shouted, and someone had his name in a twinkling.

"It's Cyclone Jones!"

"The one, the only, the inimitable!" chanted Fearless, quoting from some Wall of Death trailer.

"Up he goes, down he goes, around he goes!" cried Spark.

The skywriter was on his way north, past other bays like this one, past deeper inlets, over islands, towns, until he reached the small seaside city where he was due to hang advertisements in the sky. However, since he was a pal of Fearless' — and a member of his working team of tunnellers during the week — he had agreed to use a little of his smoke-making chemicals to give us a sample of his aerial calligraphy.

After we waved our recognition from the beach, the plane climbed higher, smoke billowing in its wake. As if blowing a smoke-ring, Cyclone Jones left a large O above us and then continued northward, wings wagging.

The strain of looking up as the O slowly thickened made the back of my neck sore, so I lay flat on the sand, shading my eyes with my hands. Soon all five of us were on our backs.

Teresa and Fearless turned and looked down on us, well pleased with the effect of the surprise, and at that moment the widening smoke-ring made a halo around their heads. It was the sort of halo that Adam and Eve might have shared before Old Nick got his pitch-fork stuck into mankind. It needed no picture-frame to convert the smoke-ring into a halo. I was wary of the square of carved and gilded wood now. It had abetted too many of my dark, murderous thoughts. Besides, it seemed childish to be peering at the world through its portals. So I went into the sandhills and dug under the stick that marked the spot where it was buried. As usual I shook it free of sand, but I did not dare raise it to the level of my eyes, because I was afraid that it might have the power to mar the peace of mind that we had found now that the reason for our rivalry existed no longer.

What should I do with it? Bury it? Leave it there? Throw away the stick that had marked its hiding-place? Yet someone might come along and find it. The winds of winter might blow away the sand and leave it exposed for someone to pick up and peer through and perhaps also be deceived. I could take it back to St Roderick's and present it to the Reverend Mother, and she might frame a print of the Holy Family in it and so make it respectable. No, I felt I should be completely rid of it. I took it to the end of the southern headland as the tide was going out and I tossed it onto the sea. It drifted down the coast as the sea darkened with evening, taking with it some of the delusions of boyhood.

The final visits were made to our haunts that day. As we passed Fingers Galore, he was out on his ledge, wriggling and twirling his fingers, but he did not curtail his miniature physical jerks until Maps spoke so loudly to us that he was bound to overhear.

"I jist seen a runaway finger."

This brought the fingers to a sudden stop as the owner held a snap roll-call and satisfied himself that all ten members were present and correct.

We found Shellback pleased to see us. This struck us as odd, and so the wariness originated with us for once.

"I'm lucky to have me own two arms still in their sockets," he announced, speaking very loudly so that his voice would carry to the one of us who hovered some distance off. "Mebbe it's a relative to Henry, a twin perhaps, but 'tis a groper t'be sure, an' no whipper-snapper either."

So Shellback seemed to be back in business, and some of the explosive saliva was on his lips again.

This brought Fido rushing forward. "Mister O'Leary!" he said with most of the twang back in his voice. "I used mussels for bait. I tried herrin's, but mussels is best."

"Ye think so, eh?"

"They're like what you said once. More potent."

"Yis, yis." Shellback nodded. "I'll make a mental note av thit. Mussels for bait. I'll keep it in me mind." But he had a shrewd and mistrustful look in his eyes which seemed to indicate that he had already made up his mind to do anything but take this particular advice.

He delivered a short farewell speech to us, his arms crossed over his leathery chest, so that he was able to stroke the furze of white hair on either shoulder as he spoke. "Well, ye've been here an' now ye're goin' away. I'll be missin' ye." This amazed us. "Yis, indade, with all ye cackle an' scurry it wuz a glimpse av the ole times again. If there's anny advice I kin give ye, each av ye, see thit ye don't grow up t'be ole fools the likes av meself." And he dismissed us for ever with a wave of his hand and set about repairing some of the heavy fishing tackle that would no doubt be welcome to catch anything except the new groper — if such a creature did exist.

There were no formal farewells from Double Martin or Sundial Watson. We spotted the former, still in the same red-and-green carpet slippers, as he stood examining his garden as if waiting for the first green shoots of the flowers to show. The wine-maker was sighted near his sundial, his mind probably at some dawn or early morning on the other side of the world. Lady Hodge remained locked up behind her high wall. Our stay at Captain's Folly was at an end and we were calmly resigned to the return to St Roderick's.

After an early breakfast on the Sunday morning, the McAnshes took their hats off the pegs and told us to pick up our belongings. On the plea that our dogs had grown so much that it would be cruel to keep them cooped up, they allowed us to remain barefooted and pack our boots in our suitcases, along with pyjamas that had been touched by moonlight, towels that had grown grubbier, and bathing-costumes that had become frail banners for their noble *Excelsior Flour* brand marks.

Men from the surf team were emerging for their first practice of the day as we passed near the back of the surf club pavilion. We had come to know each of them for some distinguishing trait: an untrained yodeller, a dedicated beer-drinker, one who was always sleepy, another who used to come out of the surf and time how long the water took to drip from his nose with a water-proof wrist-watch. They waved and nodded goodbye.

Fearless and Teresa were waiting for us near the shop. This was the first uncomfortable goodbye in our lives. Until this holiday we had never come to know anyone we might miss, except perhaps Sister Ursula, the cheer-ful nun with the agonising bunions. As the McAnshes were quick to warn us, this must be only a short stop; we must not waste time or we would miss the bus that was to take us cross-country to the city, where we were due to pick up the overnight train to the west. Fearless and Teresa shook hands with each of us. Fearless' hand was rough from his work, and so big that when it enclosed mine it included an inch of my wrist and I thought of how Teresa had almost disappeared in his Friday night embrace. We had become acquainted with the softness of Teresa's hands on our first day here. A large slice of lifetime had passed since she had first anointed us with sunburn lotion. That had been an opening ritual to an experience that was to start us on the road to manhood. With her shake came a touch on our cheeks with her other hand.

"You brought us luck," she said.

"You bet!" Fearless agreed, trying to make it easier for us, but only forcing the heartiness a little. "It prob-ably saved one of you lads from a fate worse than death.

There was a time when I thought I might have to adopt one of you."

"One?" cried Teresa, partly in consternation at his open mention of adoption.

"I did. Honest!"

"Fearless, it could never have been *one* of the boys. *All five or none at all.*"

That was a pat on the back to start each of us moving. We waved as we climbed the first leg of the zigzag, and Teresa and Fearless moved out onto the beach to be able to wave back until the hillside obscured the valley and the bay. On the second upward turn lay one of the signs we had made, its spelling still uncorrected: *Dangrous Bend.* This was a notice that might have signposted our entire nine weeks of holiday. We had come to one of life's dangerous bends, and despite the skids, slides and skirtings of evil precipices, we had negotiated it. And even though I had regarded Father Scully's counsel in the confessional as lunacy, perhaps he had bestowed some wisdom after all.

Another leg of the zigzag, and Teresa and Fearless would be cut off from our view. Down below she decided how to help us up that last stretch. She pointed at Fearless and cried up to us: "What am I offered?"

"Sixpence!" Spark yelled, catching on and moving right in. "Any advance on sixpence?"

"A shilling!" Teresa called.

We stopped, and the bidding rose into the hundreds, and then the thousands. Fearless had stepped away askance when his value was being measured in shillings, but as we advanced into the tens of thousands of pounds he began to bang himself on the chest. Near them, the horse Socrates stood with his ears sharpened. Ahead of us we had brought the McAnshes to a startled halt.

"Fifty thousand!" Teresa cried, and we decided to let

her keep him for that. Besides, the McAnshes were highly impatient.

"Hurry along, lads!"

"Time," chimed Bandy.

They had to wait a little longer.

"Going for fifty thousand pounds! Any advance on fifty thousand? Going! Going! Gone! Sold to the lady down there in the pink dress!"

Teresa sprang at her prize, and when she flung her arms around his neck her feet came off the sand.

We were about to move on and finally put the shoulder of the hill between our nine eyes and Fearless and Teresa, when the sound of a piano floated up to us.

"Upon me wretched soul!" Bandy McAnsh muttered.

Fingers Galore was thumping out "I'm Painting the Clouds with Sunshine".

Spark danced around and went through the actions of painting over his head with an imaginary brush. "I'm Painting the Clouds with Bunkum!" he sang.

"Crumbs, 'e's mad!" cried Fido. And then he made a momentous discovery about himself. *"Crumbs!"* It was a cracked twang now. " 'Eyee! Listen to me! Me voice is breakin'!"

UQP YOUNG ADULT FICTION

The Great Secondhand Supper   *Greg Bastian*

Acting on inside information about a proposed link road, Jason
Washington and his family leave the city to open a restaurant in Gum
Flats. When the road fails to appear, the Washingtons are threatened
with disaster. Jason plans to save the day by writing a prize-winning
story, "The Great Secondhand Supper", and shares his ambition with
Angela Conti, his vivacious schoolmate.

Merryll of the Stones   *Brian Caswell*

A splendid story of time travel and magic which begins in Sydney,
when Megan discovers she is the sole survivor of a motor accident. She
awakes strangely haunted by dreamlike memories. When she goes to
live in Wales, these lead her into a mystic ancient world. **Shortlisted —
Children's Book of the Year (1990) and Children's Book Award, Adelaide Festival Awards for Literature (1990).**

The Heroic Life of Al Capsella   *Judith Clarke*

Nothing is more important to fourteen-year-old Al Capsella and his
friends than being "normal". Yet despite his heroic efforts to con-
form, Al faces a crippling pair of obstacles: his mother and father.
Shortlisted — NSW Premier's Literary Awards (1989).

Al Capsella and the Watchdogs   *Judith Clarke*

Brilliant sequel to *The Heroic Life of Al Capsella*. Al and his friends
can see the end of their schooldays approaching — life is changing and
it's a bit scary. The "Watchdogs" are the anxious mothers of these
suburban teenagers; and in spite of his own Watchdog, Mrs Capsella,
Al manages to fall into some hilarious situations.

The Boy on the Lake   *Judith Clarke*
Stories of the Supernatural

In this spinechilling collection of weird and spooky stories, nothing is
as it first appears. Judith Clarke's unpredictable imagination creates a
very human world — charged with the power of mystery and the supernatural.

The Boys from Bondi   *Alan Collins*

The world of young Jacob and Solly Kaiser falls apart when they are orphaned and pitched into a Sydney children's home which is filled with refugee Jewish children from Hitler's Europe. **Shortlisted — USA National Jewish Book Award for Children's Literature (1989).**

The Inheritors   *Jill Dobson*

Twenty-five years after a nuclear war, a community of survivors live on beneath a protective dome. Sixteen-year-old Claudia, a promising youth leader, begins to question her society's oppressive values and wonder about life outside the dome's security.

Summer Press   *Rosemary Dobson*

Twelve-year-old Angela Read is left to her own devices one summer in the ancient village of Hadlow, England. She knows no one — she meets the forthright Lily, the mysterious and tragic Sarah, and a scarey silent boy.

Lonely Summers   *Nora Dugon*

Nora Dugon's appealing first novel is the story of a teenage survivor, Kelly Ryan, who befriends an impulsive elderly woman. Together this unlikely pair face excitement and danger in an inner city neighbourhood. **Shortlisted — Children's Book Award, Adelaide Festival Awards for Literature (1990).**

Clare Street   *Nora Dugon*

A sequel to *Lonely Summers:* Kelly Ryan's seventeenth year brings her first experience of love and her first taste of a settled existence within her inner-city neighbourhood.

A Season of Grannies   *James Grieve*

Of all the hair-brained schemes that Jacqui Barclay is involved with, the Rent-a-Granny enterprise is perhaps the craziest. And it leads to others, including a very peculiar relationship with Looch, the Spaghetti Eater. **Shortlisted — Guardian (UK) Children's Book of the Year Award (1988).**

McKenzie's Boots   *Michael Noonan*

Six feet four and only 15 years old — and he ran away to join the army! McKenzie and his boots went to fight the Japanese in New Guinea, finding adventure, courage and a true humanity beyond wartime propaganda. *McKenzie's Boots* was chosen for the 1988 list of Best Books for Young Adults by the Young Adult Services division of the American Library Association.

The Patchwork Hero   *Michael Noonan*

Young Hardy is the narrator of this story, set in a coastal township during the Depression of the 1930s. Hardy's mother has died; his father, Barney, is a happy-go-lucky tugboat captain — his "Patchwork Hero". One fine day Marie enters their lives — and from that moment everything changes. A new edition of this classic story of childhood, which has been successfully adapted for television.

The Other Side of the Family   *Maureen Pople*

Katharine Tucker, fifteen, is sent from England to her grandparents in Sydney to escape wartime bombing. Once there, she's sent to the bush, to the strange township and eccentric home of her legendary Grandma Tucker. Maureen Pople's first novel for teenagers has been selected as a *School Library Journal USA* Best Book of the Year (1988), and nominated for the South Carolina Young Adult Book Award (1990-1991).

Pelican Creek   *Maureen Pople*

Two teenage girls, living in a century apart, are drawn together by a secret in Maureen Pople's absorbing new novel for young adults. Living with friends in rural New South Wales while her parents' marriage breaks up, Sally Matthews finds a mysterious relic from the area's romantic past.

The Road to Summering   *Maureen Pople*

Rachel Huntley's formerly peaceful family life seems to be breaking up all around her. Her father's new partner, Caroline, and the disappearance of her brother, young George, are somehow bound up with the secret of the old house called "Summering".

Long White Cloud   *James G. Porter*

The Long White Cloud that guided the ancient Maoris to their new land is not the only cloud hanging over Gil Cook's head. His family has moved to New Zealand, to live on a small farm. When Gil leaves home intent on returning to Australia, he meets with more difficulties than he bargained for.

The Sky Between the Trees   *James Preston*

Not a book about superheroes, just a farm boy who fulfilled his ambition to become one of Australia's great axe-men. This is the stuff that Australian myths are made of.

Flight of the Albatross   *Deborah Savage*

Teenager Sarah Steinway leaves her New York home to visit her scientist mother on Great Kauri Island, New Zealand. Sarah's rescue of an injured albatross and her meeting with Mako, a Maori boy her own age, are the linked events which make her stay on the island the most memorable experience in her young life.

Blue Days   *Donna Sharp*

Marie Lucas has more than her share of the blues: her father has just died; her mother is in shock; her friends are disappointing and her boyfriend . . . Teenage life is complicated but Marie takes control at last.
Shortlisted — Children's Book of the Year (1987).